'One month,'

'What do you mean,

'That's the maximum time I reckon you'll survive here.'

She stared at him, her anger rising. How dared he assume she didn't have what it took to work in this place? Who the hell did he think he was? One month? Well, she'd do her month and more. . . She'd complete the full year, whatever it took to do so, and she'd prove Dr Harry Brolin wrong!

Laura MacDonald lives in the Isle of Wight. She is married and has a grown-up family. She has enjoyed writing fiction since she was a child, but for several years she worked for members of the medical profession, both in pharmacy and in general practice. Her daughter is a nurse and has helped with the research for Laura's medical stories.

Recent titles by the same author:

POWERS OF PERSUASION
DRASTIC MEASURES
FALSE PRETENCES

WINNING
THROUGH

BY
LAURA MACDONALD

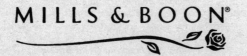

All the characters in this book have no existence outside the imagination of the author, and have no relation whatsoever to anyone bearing the same name or names. They are not even distantly inspired by any individual known or unknown to the author, and all the incidents are pure invention.

*First published in Great Britain 1997
Harlequin Mills & Boon Limited,
Eton House, 18-24 Paradise Road, Richmond, Surrey TW9 1SR*

© Laura MacDonald 1997

ISBN 0 263 80204 3

*Set in Times 10 on 11 pt. by
Rowland Phototypesetting Limited
Bury St Edmunds, Suffolk*

03-9707-49921-D

*Printed and bound in Great Britain
by Mackays of Chatham PLC, Chatham*

CHAPTER ONE

'WHY a city practice?' Kirstin had asked.

'Valuable experience,' they'd said. And she'd been prepared to go along with that, even if a little reluctantly.

She'd gone along with it when she'd packed and left her comfortable flat in her parents' house on the Isle of Wight, and gone along with it when she'd said goodbye to her friends. Even saying goodbye to Scott hadn't been as bad as she had feared in the light of this new enthusiasm.

The cautiously optimistic air had lasted throughout the ferry crossing and during the drive up the A3. Surely, she told herself as she sat in a service station and indulged in an 'all-day breakfast', life as a doctor in general practice couldn't be too much different from her work as a hospital doctor.

It had been her father who had offered to buy Kirstin a junior partnership in a local practice but, first, there was this trainee year to complete and it had been her future partners who had suggested the total change of environment.

And maybe they were right, she thought later as she negotiated the traffic on the busy M25 and headed north-east of London. Sometimes life could become a little too comfortable and it was then that some sort of challenge was required, and if Scott could go all the way to New Zealand to seek his challenge then she surely should be able to cope with this.

Her optimism was still reasonably intact when some time later she sped up the motorway in the new racing green sports car her parents had given her when she qualified and, as she approached Rawton Sunbury, it received a further boost when she stopped for coffee, then checked on her appearance.

Kirstin had dressed with great care that morning, wanting to project the right image, and as she critically surveyed her reflection in the mirror in the ladies' loo she was satisfied with what she saw. Her dark hair, cut in an attractive jaw-length bob, gleamed beneath the fluorescent light and her make-up—which accentuated her large brown eyes—she freshened up slightly, while the black suit with its long-line jacket and short skirt looked as good as when she had put it on that morning.

The area was looking pleasant, too, she thought a little later as she left the motorway, following the road as it curved and dipped under the bypass. Playing fields and parkland fresh with the promise of spring spread out on one side of the carriageway, while the other was lined with buildings which could have been anything from warehouses to small factories.

'Look for the cathedral,' a friend had told her when trying to give directions.

And suddenly there it was in front of her, dominating the skyline. Kirstin liked old churches and medieval cathedrals but this was a modern, ugly building of red brick, crouching above the city like some great brooding animal, and her first impression was one of disappointment.

That gave her the first twinge of unease, and when she took the inner city route her optimism took another dive as she passed what seemed like miles of graffiti-daubed walls, boarded-up shops and houses with rubbish-strewn gardens and doorways.

The traffic in the city centre was chaotic, the air thick with petrol fumes, but at least the shops looked promising, Kirstin thought as she searched desperately for the road signs she needed for Maybury, the area to the north of the city where the practice was.

To complete her dejection, as she left the city centre, it began to rain. It had been threatening ever since she had left London and she had watched the dark clouds gathering on the horizon.

Now it pattered noisily against the windscreen and as Kirstin flicked the switch for the wipers she pulled up at a set of traffic lights and glanced down at the direction pad on the seat beside her.

'After the fourth set of traffic lights,' she read, 'proceed to the next roundabout, then take the third exit.'

When the lights changed she drew away and found herself in a heavily built-up residential area, with old buildings on one side and on the other a vast housing estate which seemed to go on for ever with its ugly blocks of high-rise flats interspaced with vast areas of wasteland.

Had that been three or four sets of traffic lights?

She didn't know. She'd lost count. Surely she wasn't going to get lost now? Not when she was so close. No, wait a minute; here was the roundabout. Good.

She gave a signal, took the third exit and, with a sigh of relief, caught sight of a sign for Maybury. She took a quick glance at the pad beside her again. 'Second turning to the right,' the directions went on, 'then under the railway bridge, then the fourth turning to the left.'

Heavens, she thought, I'll never remember all this; I shall spend most of my time trying to find my way around.

The throng of people was the first indication of the medical centre, although Kirstin did not realise that at the time.

Her first thought when she saw such a crowd was that there had been an accident, but as she slowed the car to a crawl she quickly became aware of the curious stares of the crowd.

It was a multiracial group with the bright colours of

saris breaking the monotony of denim, leather and drab anoraks.

She was still wondering what nature of event had caused the gathering when she saw the sign: MAYBURY CITY PRACTICE. Then she knew and some inner sense, inspired no doubt by the dull expressions of the waiting individuals, warned her that this was by no means unusual and was probably a typical daily surgery.

No one moved for her to draw onto the doctors' forecourt which, surprisingly, was empty. Surely she hadn't chosen a time to arrive when there were no doctors on the premises?

In the end it was only repeated tooting of her horn that persuaded the group to shuffle aside sufficiently to enable Kirstin to drive forward and to park.

They probably think I'm a patient and jumping the queue. Kirstin smiled nervously, only too aware of the openly hostile stares as she switched off the engine and got out of her car.

The forecourt was choked with plastic bags, over-flowing with rubbish, while the walls of the building itself were covered with yet more graffiti.

No one spoke as she locked the car and made her way to the large double doors of the main entrance, which were partially covered by a forbidding-looking, iron grille.

She had to push her way through the queue as people eyed her suspiciously, before reluctantly moving aside. Fleetingly Kirstin thought of the Island practice where she would eventually be a partner—of its smart new building and its location near the marina with the tubs of flowers outside the entrance.

Then she dismissed the thought. This was not the Isle of Wight; this was Maybury, and it was unfair to compare the two.

If anything, the situation inside the building was even

worse than outside. The waiting area was jammed with people, some sitting on rows of canvas chairs and others leaning against the walls or sitting on the floor. Some were noisily demanding attention and others were silent, but all seemed to have the same empty expression on their faces as that of those in the crowd outside. A curious smell hung in the air—a mixture of damp raincoats, antiseptic and chips.

Three receptionists worked behind a glass-partitioned desk. One looked harrassed, but the other two seemed oblivious to the crowd and worked steadily, answering the telephones which rang constantly and ticking off names in a book as people reached the desk. None of them took any notice of Kirstin as she bypassed the queue and tapped on the glass.

She tapped again, louder this time, aware as she did so of a muttering behind her from a large West Indian gentleman who gave the distinct impression that he would not be pleased if he thought someone was attempting to take his place.

'Oh, it's all right,' Kirstin quickly explained. 'I'm not a patient.'

More muttering followed, as if the man could not conceive what other reason would induce anyone to be there.

A middle-aged receptionist, a rather large lady, approached the partition at that moment and peered officiously at Kirstin through the glass.

'Yes?' she demanded.

'Oh.' The word 'dragon' unwittingly entered Kirstin's mind and, as she struggled to rid herself of the image it conjured up, she was reminded of the receptionists at home and of how pleasant they were, young and attractive, while this particular lady with her severe hairstyle, horn-rimmed spectacles and intimidating expression was none of these. 'I'm looking for Dr Hardcastle,' she managed to say at last.

'Don't you mean Hardiman?' snapped the woman.

'Yes.' Kirstin frowned.

'You said Hardcastle.'

'Oh, I'm sorry, I meant Hardiman,' she said, feeling her cheeks redden. How could she have been so stupid to get his name wrong, and in front of this woman as well?

'D'you have an appointment?' the woman rapped.

'Not exactly. . . I . . .' Kirstin began, but immediately she was interrupted.

'Then you'll have to sit and wait—same as everyone else.'

Kirstin was aware of a satisfied grunt behind her then as the receptionist would have turned away she intervened hastily, tapping urgently on the glass again. 'Oh, just a minute, you don't understand,' she said. 'I'm Kirstin Patterson.'

If Kirstin thought that her name would automatically ring any bells with the woman she was sadly mistaken. Instead, with an indifferent shrug, she answered one of the endlessly ringing telephones, while behind Kirstin the muttering, taken up now by others, grew ominously louder.

In desperation she glanced round while the man behind her stepped impatiently up to the desk, pushed her to one side and gave his name to another of the receptionists who had approached the counter.

He then moved away to the congested waiting area and his place was taken by a woman with three small children who all appeared to be clinging to various parts of her anatomy.

Taking a deep breath, Kirstin deliberately stood in front of the woman to attract the attention of the second receptionist who, although younger, appeared to be just as officious as the first.

'Would you please tell Dr Hardiman that Kirstin Patterson has arrived?' she said firmly.

The girl glared at her and, as one of the children jabbed her painfully in the back, someone began screaming in the waiting area. The receptionist's attention was diverted and a nurse appeared from one of the rooms in the corridor and hurried forward.

Kirstin quickly realised that it was not the hysterical woman who was in trouble but her companion—another, much younger, obese woman—who had fallen to the floor and was twitching and jerking uncontrollably.

Kirstin automatically turned and hurried to help, dropping to her knees and attempting to hold the young woman to prevent her from harming herself while the nurse checked that her airway was clear.

'Thank you. . . Help me turn her,' gasped the nurse, who was struggling with the sheer weight of the woman.

They had just manoeuvred the patient, who by this time had slipped into unconsciousness, into the recovery position when someone began shouting.

'Right, come on. Stand back there. Let me through.'

Kirstin, still on her knees on the linoleum, wet from the raincoats, looked up. Her first impression was of an untidy man with a surly, bad-tempered expression.

The nurse also looked up. 'This lady has helped,' she said crisply, indicating Kirstin.

'Good. Right. Thank you,' said the man. 'But I'm here now. If you'll stand back, please.'

Kirstin scrambled to her feet, aware as she did so that her tights had gone into holes at the knees and that there was dirt on her skirt and on the front of her jacket.

Moving aside, she watched as the man took charge.

Was this Dr Hardiman?

She had no means of knowing as all arrangements with the man who was to be her trainer had been carried out over the telephone. But even as the question crossed her mind she found herself hoping that this man wasn't he.

She wasn't sure why; she just knew that there was something about him she had taken an instant dislike to.

And for the next fifteen minutes or so, as she watched the emergency being dealt with and an ambulance being sent for, Kirstin found very little about him that would persuade her to change that opinion.

She judged him to be somewhere in his late thirties, not particularly tall and certainly not handsome—his features rugged and uneven—of slightly stocky build and with untidy dark hair that kept falling into his eyes. He was not wearing a jacket and he'd rolled up his shirtsleeves to the elbow, revealing a covering of dark hair on his arms. Something about this disturbed Kirstin and she found herself looking away.

She had long since decided that it was not a good time to pursue her case, and while she resigned herself to waiting the queue of patients grew steadily longer.

Other staff appeared briefly, before retreating to their rooms again. One, a thin, anxious-looking man slightly older than the one attending the epileptic patient but without his short-tempered manner, was presumably another doctor. Kirstin found herself hoping that out of the two perhaps he might be Dr Hardiman.

The reception staff seemed completely unfazed by the drama and carried on with their work as if nothing was happening. The patient's companion continued to have hysterics and was eventually dealt with, none too gently, by the surly-faced doctor.

Kirstin was just wondering if anyone would ever know if she simply melted away and drove straight back to the Isle of Wight ferry when the ambulance arrived and two paramedics fought their way through the crowd.

The patient, who by that time had regained consciousness, was duly secured into a chair and, escorted by the doctor, was wheeled outside to the waiting ambulance.

The hubbub in the waiting area gradually subsided and

Kirstin was just wondering if she dared approach anyone again when there was a further commotion and the surly-faced doctor strode back into the reception area, shouting and waving his arms.

'Which idiot left that sports car on the forecourt?' he demanded, glaring round.

The waiting people mumbled, shook their heads and averted their eyes.

'Because whoever did,' the doctor went on, 'will soon find it minus its wheels.' He was breathing heavily and it was quite obvious that his surliness had erupted into anger.

Kirstin swallowed and stepped forward. 'It's my car,' she said, and in the silence that followed she was only too aware that not only had the doctor turned to her, but that the eyes of everyone in the place had turned in her direction.

'Yours?' The doctor stared at her. His hair had become even more untidy during the episode with the patient and now hung down over his forehead. 'What in hell possessed you to leave it there?'

'It said "Doctors' Car Park". . .' Kirstin began, aware that her face had flushed under so many curious stares.

'Exactly!' Sarcasm was added to the anger now.

In that moment of scrutiny and humiliation—as she faced the man across the crowded room and someone tittered behind her—Kirstin hated him. 'So I considered I qualified. . .' she continued, aware now that his eyes had narrowed. 'I'm Kirstin Patterson,' she concluded at last. 'Dr Patterson.'

He continued to stare at her, his expression impossible to read. 'I can assure you that won't make a lot of difference,' he said at last. 'Believe me, the fact you are a doctor will offer no protection.'

'But. . .' She frowned, bewildered.

'Come with me,' he rapped, turning away.

Kirstin glanced round, angry at his attitude. She'd been prepared to overlook his manner when he hadn't known her identity, but now there was no excuse for his rudeness. But if she'd thought that she would receive support from anyone else she was mistaken for, all around her, the stares—whether from staff or patients—if not exactly hostile, were totally indifferent.

Fighting the anger which was threatening to boil over, Kirstin forced her way through the crowd again and followed the man outside.

Somehow, miraculously, the crowd parted when they saw the doctor, albeit reluctantly and with renewed muttering, but then Kirstin's newly acquired sense of balance was brutally thrown by her companion's sudden furious shout.

'Bugger off, you lot!'

Momentarily she was shocked. Where she came from doctors quite simply didn't speak to patients in that fashion. Then, as she turned the corner of the building and the doctors' car park came into view, she saw the reason for his outburst.

Her car—her pride and joy—still the only vehicle on the patch, was surrounded by four youths. One was fiddling with a doorhandle, while another was crouched down beside the near side front wheel. They all appeared to be dressed in the same dark donkey jackets, jeans and knitted woollen hats pulled low over their foreheads.

As the doctor strode across the car park towards them they straightened up, eyeing him. Kirstin felt her outrage replaced by a tight knot of fear somewhere in the pit of her stomach.

'Go on, beat it!' shouted the doctor. 'They'll already have called the cops.' He jerked his head towards the building behind him. 'So clear off!'

The line of patients carried on shuffling forward, as if

what was happening was commonplace and certainly no cause for speculation.

Kirstin stood frozen to the spot as the young men continued to eye her and the doctor up and down and then, to her utmost relief, they began to back away warily until eventually they turned and ran down the street, finally disappearing round a corner.

'Oh, thank God!' she breathed.

'Got your keys?'

'I'm sorry?'

'Your car keys.' He sounded impatient, exasperated even.

'Oh, yes, yes, of course.' Kirstin fumbled inside her leather shoulder-bag, found her bunch of keys and was about to unlock her car when she realised that the doctor was holding out his hand. Meekly she found herself handing over the keys. Now was obviously not the time to argue.

He unlocked the car and slid into the driver's seat. 'Get in,' he snapped.

Kirstin, aware of the now curious stares of the crowd, walked round the car and opened the passenger door. He had started the engine before she was inside, and was reversing before she had time even to slam the door.

She wanted to ask him where they were going but didn't quite dare. His tight-lipped silence was almost as terrifying as the menacing attitude of the gang of youths.

He reversed the car out of the car park onto the road then drove forward, before turning into the entrance of an alleyway that ran alongside the building. At the end of the alley they were confronted by a set of gates, constructed of heavy metal mesh and bound with a large padlock.

Leaving the engine running, the doctor leapt from the car, took a bunch of keys from his trouser pocket and unlocked the gates—pushing them back to allow room for him to drive the car forward.

As he resumed his seat and drove forward Kirstin found that they were in some sort of compound constructed entirely of the same heavy mesh as the doors but having not only walls but a roof as well. There were about half a dozen other cars in the compound, and as Kirstin gazed around her in amazement she heard a dry chuckle.

She threw a startled glance at her companion. A laugh or even a smile was the last thing she would have expected from him but his expression, although not exactly pleasant, had indeed lightened.

'Welcome to the staff car park of Maybury City Practice,' he said.

He must have sensed her startled bewilderment for, before she had the chance to comment, he added, 'All this is very necessary, I can assure you.'

'But. . .'

He cut her short. 'Like I said, a few more minutes and they would have had your radio, then the wheels. It's happened to all of us,' he went on in case she needed any further convincing.

Helplessly, in silence, she glanced around and above her at the strong mesh of the enclosure.

'We had this compound erected about a year ago,' her companion said after a moment, 'after Dr Hardiman was called out on an emergency and found his car had practically been demolished. When he eventually got to the house he'd been called to, in a police car, it was to find the patient—a four-year-old child—had died ten minutes earlier. That was the turning point. That was when we decided we couldn't let them win any longer.' He paused and would have continued, but Kirstin intervened.

'So you're not Dr Hardiman?' she said.

He shook his head. 'Good God, no.'

Kirstin felt a wave of emotion flow through her. At first she wasn't sure what it was then, after a further quick glance at the man beside her, she recognised it as relief. Relief that it wasn't he who was to be her trainer.

Briefly, almost as if he had read her thoughts, his eyes met hers. They were a strange colour, she thought, neither brown nor hazel but a sort of tawny colour.

'Come on,' he said abruptly, 'I'll take you to meet Charles.'

Opening the car door, he got out and waited impatiently while Kirstin did the same then retrieved her briefcase from the boot. After locking the car, he tossed her the keys and together they walked out of the compound.

'So you're Charles's trainee?' He locked the compound and pocketed his keys.

'Yes.' Kirstin nodded. There was something about this man that still made her feel very uncomfortable.

'Glutton for punishment, Charles.' He gave a sound somewhere between a snort and a grunt.

'I beg your pardon?' said Kirstin coldly as they began to walk back up the alley to the road.

'As if we don't have enough problems here, he will keep taking trainees.'

'Someone has to, I suppose,' Kirstin replied in the same cool tones.

'It wouldn't be so bad if they stayed,' he retorted.

'What do you mean?' Kirstin threw him a wary glance.

'Well, none of them do. They can't cope. Three months was the longest anyone stayed—and he was a tough guy—Welsh Rugby champ but it even got to him in the end.'

Kirstin remained silent. She could guess what he was thinking—that she wouldn't be any different. And, from what she'd seen so far, she was indeed wondering how long she would survive in these conditions, but she wasn't going to give him the satisfaction of voicing her concerns.

By this time they had reached the forecourt and once again had to force their way through the crowd.

'Is it always like this?' she asked briefly as they finally got through into Reception.

'Always.' His reply, tossed casually over his shoulder, was abrupt.

Nothing appeared to have changed inside. The receptionists still answered phones and dealt with the never-ending stream of patients, while the sheer volume of people in the waiting area seemed, if anything, to have increased instead of lessened.

Somehow Kirstin found herself on the other side of the glass partition where the officious-looking receptionist who had earlier dismissed her very existence now critically eyed her up and down.

'Eva, this is Kirstin Patterson—Dr Hardiman's new trainee,' explained her companion.

'Why didn't you say?' demanded the woman.

'I tried to. . .' Kirstin began, but no one was listening. The woman had lifted a receiver and punched out a number and the doctor had been waylaid by another receptionist, frantically demanding that he sign a prescription.

'Dr Hardiman will see you now.' The woman banged down the receiver and turned to the partition where someone was hammering on the glass. 'You can cut that out,' she barked.

'I'll take you through.' The doctor spoke, without looking up, as he scribbled on a prescription pad.

'Dr Brolin?' Another receptionist approached him. 'Are you doing an antenatal clinic tomorrow?'

He nodded in reply, tore off the prescription, tossed it at the other receptionist then gestured for Kirstin to follow him.

So that was his name, thought Kirstin as she followed the solid, arrogant figure down the corridor.

Brolin. Dr Brolin.

Thank God he wasn't to be her trainer, she thought and then, as they stopped before a door which bore the name of Charles Hardiman, she found herself dreading what she might find. Maybe Charles Hardiman would be worse than Dr Brolin.

Somehow she doubted it.

She watched as he tapped on the door, opened it, stuck his head round, said something then stood back for her to enter the room.

The man behind the desk who turned to face her was in his sixties and, with his thick white hair and kindly expression, presented a definite fatherly image.

With an inward sigh of relief Kirstin held out her hand.

'Kirstin, my dear.' Charles Hardiman moved round the desk and took her hand. 'You're earlier than I expected. Did you have a good journey?'

'Yes, pretty good, thank you,' Kirstin replied, aware that Dr Brolin was still hovering in the doorway. 'At least I didn't get lost.'

'You drove up?' Charles Hardiman sounded surprised then, when Kirstin nodded, he glanced at his colleague. 'Kirstin's home is on the Isle of Wight, Harry,' he explained. 'She is to be a partner eventually in Hamish Forbes's practice. Hamish is an old friend and colleague.'

'When she's completed her trainee year, presumably?' There was an edge to Harry Brolin's voice, an edge which Kirstin would probably not have detected but for the incident that had just occurred, but which she now recognised as scepticism.

'Well, yes, of course,' replied Charles aimiably. 'That's why she's come to us, isn't it, Kirstin?'

'Yes.' Somehow she managed a smile.

'Are you fixed up with accommodation?' Harry Brolin

asked the question suddenly, unexpectedly.

Kirstin wished that he would just go and leave her to talk to Charles Hardiman. It wasn't as if he didn't have plenty to do, for heaven's sake, she thought, recalling the hordes of waiting people, but Harry Brolin seemed unperturbed and in no immediate hurry.

'Kirstin is staying with Estelle and me to start with.' It was Charles who answered. 'Just until she finds herself a flat or something. . .' He broke off as the phone rang. 'Excuse me a moment.' He picked up the receiver, put it to his ear and, turning towards the window, listened then began discussing what was obviously a case history.

'The Isle of Wight, eh?' Harry Brolin, still apparently in no hurry to leave, stared at her with what Kirstin thought was renewed interest.

'Yes,' she nodded, then looked away.

'So, what do you do down there?'

'My parents live there,' she replied coolly. 'It's my home.'

'Is your father a doctor?'

She shook her head. 'No, he's a managing director in our family firm of boat-builders.'

'Ah,' he murmured softly. 'Little Miss Rich Girl.'

'I beg your pardon.' She looked up sharply but the hard, rugged face was expressionless.

'One month,' he replied softly.

'What do you mean, one month?' Kirstin frowned.

'That's how long I give you.'

'What. . .?'

'That's the maximum time I reckon you'll survive here.'

She stared at him, her anger rising, then—as Charles finished his conversation and replaced the receiver— Harry Brolin suddenly winked and, backing out of the room, shut the door.

Kirstin stared after him. That hadn't been a friendly

wink. Far from it. It had been almost unpleasant.

How dared he? How dared he assume she didn't have what it took to work in this place? Who the hell did he think he was?

Well, she'd show him. She'd jolly well show him.

One month? Was that what he'd said? Was that the amount of time he'd given her? Well, she'd do her month and more. . .much more. . . She'd complete the full year, whatever it took to do so, and she'd prove Dr Harry Brolin wrong!

CHAPTER TWO

HALF an hour later Kirstin found herself in the doctors'
staffroom, drinking a much-needed cup of coffee while
Charles Hardiman finished his surgery.

'Time enough for you to enter the fray tomorrow,'
he'd said, 'and, besides, you must be in need of refresh-
ment after your journey.'

The coffee was surprisingly good and Kirstin had just
helped herself to a second cup when the staffroom door
opened and the nurse she had seen earlier in Reception
came into the room.

'Oh, I'm sorry. I didn't know there was anyone in
here,' she said when she caught sight of Kirstin, and
added, 'Oh, it's you!' She had a foreign accent and her
hair and eyes, not unlike Kirstin's own, were very dark.

'Yes,' said Kirstin quickly. 'Please come in. I was told
to help myself to coffee,' she added then, seeing the
woman's slightly puzzled expression, she said, 'I'm
Kirstin Patterson—the new trainee.'

'Oh, I see.' The nurse's features relaxed into a smile.
'That accounts for you knowing what to do out there.
Pleased to meet you. I'm Isabella Fedora—
practice nurse.'

They shook hands then Isabella poured herself a coffee
and said, 'I'm sure we can find some biscuits to go
with this.'

Kirstin watched, sipping her own coffee, as the nurse
crossed the room, unlocked a small cupboard and took
out a tin.

'Yes.' Isabella smiled over her shoulder. 'Here we are,
Custard Creams or Bourbons?'

'Oh, a Bourbon, please,' said Kirstin. 'They've always been my favourites. . . But, tell me, does everything have to be locked up around here?'

'Locked up?' Isabella frowned.

'Well, first the staff cars. . .now the biscuits.'

'Oh, I see.' Isabella laughed. 'I'm afraid so.' She gave a rueful shrug as she passed the tin to Kirstin. 'When did you arrive?' she asked.

'About half an hour ago.'

'So, who have you met?'

'I saw a rather straight-faced lady in Reception. . .'

Isabella gave a peal of laughter. 'Oh, that's Eva. Eva Sansome. You must not mind Eva. Her bark is much, much worse than her bite. . .'

'I'll take your word for it,' replied Kirstin drily, before biting into her biscuit.

'Eva is a very useful person to have around this place,' said Isabella seriously. 'When there is trouble we send for Eva, and she sorts it out.'

'I see.' Kirstin nodded but thought that she would probably need a little more convincing of that for, while she could imagine Eva being an asset where muscle power was needed, she doubted her diplomatic skills.

'What about doctors. . .have you met any doctors? Charles. . .he is to be your trainer?'

'Yes,' Kirstin nodded. 'And, yes, I have met him.'

'Charles is a sweetie,' said Isabella. 'He's getting a bit forgetful these days, but he really is a sweetie.'

'Yes, I thought he seemed really nice,' agreed Kirstin. She paused and said, 'Oh, and I've also met Dr Brolin.'

There must have been some inadvertent inflection in her voice for Isabella looked up sharply. 'You've met Harry? Apart from that business with the patient, I mean?'

Kirstin nodded and pulled a face. 'Yes, there was a

rather unfortunate incident in the car park which he sorted out for me.'

'Oh, it was you on the end of that commotion, was it?' Isabella looked at her with renewed interest.

'Yes, unfortunately I'd parked my car on the forecourt where it received some unwanted attention. . .but. . .'

'You weren't to know,' said Isabella.

'Try telling that to Dr Brolin,' replied Kirstin crisply.

'You mustn't mind Harry,' said Isabella. 'He can be very short-tempered at times. . .'

'Another one whose bark is worse than his bite?' Kirstin raised her eyebrows and with one finger wiped biscuit crumbs from the corner of her mouth.

Isabella laughed. 'Perhaps you could say that.—I'm not really sure—I would imagine Harry can bite as well as bark—but one thing I do know is that he's a very good doctor.'

'Really?' Kirstin, remembering the way he had spoken to the gang of youths, decided that was another fact of which she might need more convincing.

'There are two other doctors for you to meet,' said Isabella, 'Bruce Courtney and Rhannie Bannergee. You may see them later after surgery.'

'I expect I shall,' agreed Kirstin. 'Dr Hardiman is calling a staff meeting.'

'That's good.' Isabella drained her cup and stood up. 'I must get back now.' She paused. 'Would you like me to show you round the treatment rooms and then you can meet Val Metcalf—she's the other practice nurse?'

'Yes, please. I would like that.' Kirstin rose. Anything was better than just sitting around in the staffroom, waiting for surgery to end.

Val Metcalf was a plump, motherly type of woman in her late thirties, about ten years older than both Isabella and Kirstin. She seemed pleased that Kirstin had joined the team.

'It'll be nice to have another pair of hands around the place,' she said as Isabella conducted Kirstin around the small but well-equipped treatment rooms.

Kirstin observed for a while as the two nurses resumed their clinic and dealt with several patients then, when the going became a bit frantic, she offered to collect some records from reception for Val Metcalf for a woman who was demanding that her child be seen at the same time as herself.

To Kirstin's relief, there was no sign of the officious Eva in Reception. Isabella might well have said that the woman's bark was far worse than her bite but Kirstin was not at that particular moment inclined to put the theory to the test. Instead, she found that she had a pert-faced teenager, complete with a strong Cockney accent, to deal with.

'All right, then?' The girl grinned at Kirstin. 'You're the new trainee, ain't ya?'

'Yes,' Kirstin agreed, 'I am. Who are you?'

'Hayley,' said the girl, 'Hayley Banks.'

'Well, Hayley,' said Kirstin, 'perhaps you'd be good enough to find the records of this child for Sister Metcalf—his name is Jake Masters.'

'Right, hang on a minute.' The girl disappeared into the record section. Kirstin gazed out into the waiting area and was just thinking that the crowd at last seemed to be lessening when a voice at her elbow made her jump.

'Have they got you working already?'

She turned sharply and found Harry Brolin beside her.

'Not really,' she said shortly. 'I simply decided to make myself useful, that's all.'

'So, when do you intend doing some proper work?'

There was a definite touch of sarcasm in his tone now and Kirstin stiffened. 'Dr Hardiman said tomorrow,' she replied abruptly, at the same time wondering what it was about this man that seemed to set her on edge every time she had any contact with him.

'I suppose you'll be sitting in on Charles's surgeries.' Harry Brolin leaned across the desk and scrutinised the appointment book.

'That's the general idea,' Kirstin agreed.

'Let's hope the excitement won't prove too much for you,' he murmured. 'Charles doesn't exactly hold the wildest of consultations these days.'

'I'm sure I shall cope,' she replied coldly, glaring at him and thinking what an objectionable man he was. Then, as Hayley came up and handed her the child's records, to Kirstin's further annoyance he peered over her shoulder to read the name on the envelope.

'Jake Masters?' he almost barked. 'He's my patient. What are you doing with his records?'

Kirstin's chin went up. She refused to let this man intimidate her. 'Sister Metcalf asked me to fetch them,' she replied calmly.

'What for?'

'She has just treated the boy's mother and the woman asked if she would look at her son at the same time.'

'What's wrong with him?'

'The child was complaining of earache—but I'm sure Sister Metcalf can cope. . .'

'The boy's prone to ear infections. He'll need an antibiotic. I'd better go and have a look at him.' Not even bothering to take the records, he strode off down the corridor—leaving Kirstin and Hayley staring after him.

The receptionist must have caught sight of Kirstin's expression for she raised her eyebrows and said, 'Bit soon for your clash with Dr Brolin.'

'What do you mean?' Kirstin threw the girl a sharp glance.

'Well, everyone has one sooner or later,' she said with

a shrug, 'and it don't take long as a rule, but this is extra quick, I must say.'

'It doesn't bother me,' said Kirstin, trying to remain cool and unconcerned. 'And neither, for that matter, does Dr Brolin.'

'Don't he?' Hayley raised her eyebrows. 'Don't you fancy him, then?'

'Certainly not!' retorted Kirstin. 'He's definitely not my type.'

'Well, he can have the top off my egg any time he likes.' Hayley grinned.

Kirstin stared at the girl in amazement. She would have thought that Harry Brolin was the last person who would have appealed to a girl like Hayley but, then, she supposed, there was no accounting for taste.

As Hayley went back into Reception to answer yet another ringing telephone Kirstin glanced helplessly down at the set of records in her hand. No doubt they would still be needed. Even if the boy was Harry Brolin's patient and he was given an antibiotic it would still need to be entered into the records. Kirstin wasn't too familiar with the procedures of general practice, having spent almost the entire time of her training inside a teaching hospital, but she did know that a record had to be kept of any form of treatment. With a sigh she made her way back to the treatment room.

Dr Brolin was examining the boy's ears while the mother bombarded him with a barrage of questions. Kirstin crossed the room and handed the records to Val Metcalf.

'Did you ask him to come in?' Val muttered under her breath as she took the records.

'No, of course not,' Kirstin replied in the same low tones. 'He asked me what I was doing, and when he saw the notes he. . .'

But Val Metcalf wasn't listening. Instead, she took the

boy's records across the treatment room and stood beside
Harry Brolin as he finished his examination.

Kirstin sighed. She really didn't seem to be getting off
to a very good start with anyone. It now looked as if
even Val Metcalf thought she had interfered. As she
turned away she caught Isabella's eye. The sister smiled
sympathetically at her.

'Right, Jake.' Dr Brolin had been crouching beside the
child and now stood up. 'Bit of infection there,' he said
to the boy's mother. 'I'll give an antibiotic but I'll want
to see him again at the end of the course. Make an
appointment, please, on your way out for a week's time.
See you, then, old chap.' He ruffled Jake's hair, took his
records then began writing a prescription and entering
up the treatment.

As the boy and his mother left the room Val said, 'I
would have asked her to make an appointment for Jake
if I'd thought it necessary.'

'Sure.' Harry Brolin nodded. 'But the sooner he starts
his treatment the better. Now, I understand we have a
staff meeting?' He glanced at his wrist-watch as
she spoke.

When no one answered he moved to the door then
glanced back at Kirstin. 'Better make sure you're there,'
he said. 'I would imagine it's for your benefit.'

The door swung to behind him and Kirstin turned to
Val Metcalf. 'I hope you didn't think I—'

'Forget it.' Val shrugged and, turning away, began
clearing up the equipment and dressings she'd
been using.

'But,' Kirstin continued, 'I didn't have any choice;
he. . .'

'I said forget it,' Val said again. She didn't sound
exactly annoyed, just offhand, but the warmth that had
been in her voice earlier had disappeared.

Miserably Kirstin turned away, left the treatment room

and made her way back through Reception to the staffroom.

Charles Hardiman was already there and he looked up from the journal he was reading as Kirstin came into the room.

'Oh, there you are,' he said. 'I wondered where you'd got to. Been familiarising yourself with the place and what goes on here?'

Kirstin nodded. 'You could say that.'

Charles frowned and appeared to be on the point of asking her if there was anything wrong when the door opened and the rest of the staff began to arrive.

They were soon talking and laughing with each other with the easy familiarity that is inevitable between close colleagues, and Kirstin suddenly wished that she was somewhere else. It didn't really matter where—whether at home with her family and friends or at the hospital where she'd completed her training. She just knew that she didn't want to be here in this awful place with these people she didn't know and probably wasn't going to like, and who, if today had been anything to go by, probably weren't going to like her either.

'Thank you all for coming.' Charles was talking and Kirstin forced herself to concentrate. 'As you will appreciate, we have a new member of staff in our midst and the purpose of this gathering is for you to meet her and for us all to welcome her to the Maybury practice. This, everyone, is Kirstin Patterson.'

A polite murmur rippled round the room and out of the corner of her eye Kirstin saw the door open again and Harry Brolin come into the room. He closed the door and leaned against it.

'Kirstin will be here for one year.' Charles was speaking again. 'She will be working with me for most of the time but I hope the rest of you will give her all the support and encouragement you can.' He cleared his throat. 'Kirstin comes to us from her home on the Isle of Wight and I'm sure she is going to find life here rather different from what she is used to. . .'

'You can say that again,' said a voice from the back.

'I used to spend holidays on the Isle of Wight when I was a child,' said another voice from the far side of the room. 'I didn't know it was still there.'

In the laughter that followed Kirstin looked up and recognised the thin-faced doctor she'd seen earlier in Reception. 'I can assure you it is,' she said. 'We've lost a few chunks into the sea in recent years but there's still plenty left.'

'Kirstin, this is Bruce Courtney,' said Charles then, as the doctor crossed the room and Kirstin shook hands with him, he went on, 'Now, let's see, Harry you've already met. . .'

Kirstin looked up and as her gaze met Harry Brolin's he inclined his head.

'. . .and this, of course, is Rhannie. . . Dr Bannergee comes to us from Calcutta.'

She was quite, quite beautiful, Kirstin thought, in her saffron-coloured sari with its silver edging, the deep red cast mark on her forehead and with her black hair in a thick plait that hung down her back, almost reaching her waist.

The nurses and reception staff had also crowded into the staffroom and Kirstin became quite confused by the names and faces, some, like Isabella and Val, whom she'd already met—and Eva and Hayley—but still others whom she hadn't—other receptionists and ancillary staff.

Then, before she knew where she was, Charles was telling her that they hoped she would be happy working with them and then the throng was clearing as the staff prepared to go home.

'I used to go to Sandown.' Bruce Courtney was suddenly by her side. 'I remember playing on the beach there and fishing from the end of the pier. There was a canoe lake, too, if I remember rightly. My brother fell in once. . . Is that where you live—Sandown?'

'No.' Kirstin smiled and shook her head. 'No, I live at a place called Bembridge, but I know Sandown well.'

'You've brought back memories.' Bruce shook his head. 'Maybe I'll take my kids down there for a weekend and show them where their dad used to play when he was their age.'

He didn't look like a Bruce, Kirstin thought as he nodded and left the room. To her, the name Bruce conjured up an image of a large, affable, bearded man—the exact opposite of Dr Courtney, who was slightly built and clean-shaven and who seemed to have a permanently anxious expression.

She turned her head and looked at Harry Brolin and as the words 'street fighter' flashed unbidden into her mind Kirstin decided that, with his stocky build, slightly aggressive manner, his rugged features and the deep shadow on his jaw, his name suited him admirably.

'I suggest, Kirstin, that you follow me. I think that will be easier than me trying to give you directions.'

'Yes, of course, Charles.' Kirstin opened her car door and slid into the driver's seat, while Charles Hardiman climbed into a rather elderly Volvo.

On the far side of the compound Harry Brolin had just started up the engine of a large, dark Citroën so covered in dust and grime that it was almost impossible to tell its colour.

Charles drew out of the compound first, raising his hand to Harry, then Kirstin drove out—studiously looking ahead and avoiding Harry Brolin's gaze. It was only when she drew up behind Charles as he waited at the end of the alley to pull out into the road that she allowed herself a quick glance in her driving mirror.

By then Harry had also driven out of the compound and as his had been the only car left he had got out, leaving his engine running, and was securing the padlock on the heavy mesh gates.

She watched him. He was not a particularly tall man but his body looked muscular, powerful, while his movements were surprisingly lithe, almost panther-like. With his dark jacket, its collar turned up against the chill March wind, he didn't look unlike one of the gang who had tried to break into her car.

Before he got back into his car, almost as if he sensed that Kirstin was watching him, he looked up and stared towards the rear of her car. Hastily she looked away. The last thing she wanted was that he should think she was watching him; was interested in some way.

Moments later she became uncomfortably aware that his car had drawn forward and that he was right behind her. Carefully she avoided looking in her mirror again. Then, to her relief, Charles at last drew out into the stream of traffic and she was able to follow him.

The evening traffic was heavy but somehow Kirstin managed to stay with Charles's Volvo, and on the occasions she looked in her rear-view mirror it was to find that the Citroën was also still behind them.

It had stopped raining but the roads were still wet and driving conditions were made difficult by a combination of the gathering dusk and the shimmering reflection of lights on the wet road surface.

Kirstin had no idea where Charles lived but he seemed to be driving right out of the Maybury area, leaving behind them the vast housing complexes with their tower blocks and the depressing rows of partially boarded-up shops and houses.

The area they were entering seemed very different— the roads narrower and tree-lined, the houses larger and set in gardens behind well-tended hedges.

Kirstin wasn't sure at what point they lost the Citroën. She only knew that at one time when she looked in her mirror it wasn't there. She wasn't sure what she felt— relief that he had gone but which, at the same time, was curiously tinged with regret that she had somehow missed the moment of his going.

And that, she told herself sharply, was ridiculous. Why in the world should it matter to her whether Harry Brolin was around or not? The man had already proved to be nothing but a source of irritation, even if he had saved her car from vandalism, and all she should be doing was thanking her lucky stars that it was Charles Hardiman who was her trainer and not his partner.

The next moment all thoughts of Harry Brolin were swept from her mind as Charles signalled a right turn and drew across the road into the spacious drive of a large, white house set well back from the road and sur- rounded by a variety of conifers.

'Well, here we are.' Charles got out of his car and turned to Kirstin as she opened her door. 'Welcome to Fir Tree Lodge. Come along inside and meet my wife.'

Estelle Hardiman, a youthful sixty, tall and elegant, proved to be as charming as her husband, and very soon Kirstin had settled into a pretty guest bedroom on the first floor, had unpacked, taken a shower and joined her hosts for a pre-dinner drink.

'So you are to go into partnership with Hamish?' said Estelle as they sipped their sherry.

'As a very junior partner,' protested Kirstin.

'Maybe so.' Estelle inclined her head. 'But your future is secure and that is no mean consideration these days.'

'I have my trainee year to get through first.' Kirstin smiled and glanced at Charles.

'It'll be dreadful. He's a tyrant, you know.' Estelle smiled at her husband who pulled a face at her.

'Oh, I know. I could tell that the moment I met him.'

Kirstin went along with the pretence. 'I'm dreading it, I can tell you.'

They all laughed at that, then Estelle grew serious. 'It won't all be plain sailing though, Kirstin, not in Maybury.'

'No, I have rather gathered that.' Kirstin set her glass down.

'Kirstin was the victim of would-be vandals the moment she set foot in the place.' explained Charles.

'Really?' Estelle looked concerned and her husband continued.

'She parked on the forecourt and her car was, shall we say, the object of some unwanted attention.'

'Oh, dear, what happened?'

'Harry came to her rescue and, in his own indomitable way, he dealt with the situation as only Harry can.'

'Good for Harry.' Estelle gave a low chuckle then, glancing at Kirstin, she said, 'And what did you think of our Dr Brolin, Kirstin?'

'I'm not sure, really,' Kirstin replied. 'I'm inclined to think it was a case of the lesser of two evils—between him and the vandals.'

They all laughed again but at that moment the telephone rang and with a sigh Charles got up to answer it.

'You're not on call, are you?' asked Estelle.

'No, that's Bruce's pleasure tonight,' Charles replied, before disappearing into the hall.

'You've met Bruce?' asked Estelle as the door closed behind her husband.

'Yes.' Kirstin nodded. 'And Rhannie. I gather Bruce has a family. What about Rhannie?'

Estelle shook her head. 'No, Rhannie doesn't have children, although she is married—to Sanjay, another doctor; he works at the hospital.'

'And what about Harry Brolin? Is he married?' Kirstin didn't really know why she'd asked. . . It wasn't as if she really wanted to know but, nevertheless, she found herself waiting for Estelle's reply.

'No, Harry isn't married,' she said at last.

'I doubt anyone would have him,' replied Kirstin lightly.

Estelle stared at her in a slightly amused fashion. 'Poor Harry really has made a bad impression, hasn't he?'

Kirstin shrugged and Estelle went on. 'He's not all bad, you know. Oh, I know his manner can be abrasive at times, but there's another side. . . And, as for no one wanting him, well, I think it will take a special kind of woman to finally catch Harry.'

'Where does he live?' Choosing to ignore what Estelle had just said, Kirstin was suddenly intrigued as to exactly where it had been that they had lost the Citroën.

'He has an apartment down near the docks.'

Kirstin had a brief vision of one of the huge concrete tower blocks they'd passed earlier, but she was saved from further comment as Charles at that moment came back into the room.

'That was Juliet.' He was smiling as he spoke. 'Our daughter,' he explained to Kirstin. 'She phoned to say that Matthew, our grandson, has been chosen for his school rugby team.'

'Oh, that's wonderful.' Estelle jumped to her feet. 'So not only are we celebrating Kirstin's arrival but Matthew's success as well. I think this calls for a bottle of wine with our meal, Charles.'

Gradually, throughout the evening, Kirstin felt herself relax. The Hardimans were the type of people she was used to, their lifestyle similar to the one she lived at home.

By the time she went to bed she was feeling much happier about her forthcoming year at the Maybury clinic and before she fell asleep, in spite of the traumatic day she'd spent and the predictions of Harry Brolin that she wouldn't last five minutes, Kirstin found herself actually looking forward to the next day when she would take her place beside Charles in his surgery.

Maybe she'd been wrong. Maybe things weren't going to be as bad as she'd feared. She didn't know. But, whatever, she was prepared to give it a chance.

CHAPTER THREE

'AH, MRS SELBY. Good morning. Now this is Dr Patterson. Do you have any objection if she stays in the room?'

The rather tired-looking woman wearily shook her head and sat down.

'Right, then, now let me see. You've been to the hospital recently, haven't you?' Charles Hardiman pulled out a wad of letters from the woman's record envelope and began scanning the most recent ones.

Kirstin smiled at Mrs Selby and was met with a blank stare.

'Ah, yes, that's right,' Charles said after a few moments. 'I have a reply from the consultant gynaecologist. Now, you saw him, what, a fortnight ago?'

The woman continued to look blank. 'No.' She shook her head. 'I saw Mr Blaine.'

'Yes, that's right.' Charles looked over his glasses at her and nodded. 'Mr Blaine is the consultant gynaecologist.' He paused. 'Now, he is in agreement with me that you are suffering from a condition known as endometriosis. . .which is inflammation of the lining of your womb.'

The woman looked up sharply. 'He said an operation. . .' she began.

'That's right.' Charles nodded. 'He says. . .' he glanced at the letter in his hands '. . .a hysterectomy in the near future. . .and that, Mrs Selby, should be the end of all the troubles and the pain you've been experiencing.'

'I don't know about this operation.' Mrs Selby frowned

and Kirstin, looking up, saw the fear in her eyes.

'There's nothing whatsoever to be afraid of...' Charles began rummaging around on his desk. 'There are some leaflets around somewhere explaining all about hysterectomy...wait a minute... Oh, they seem to have all gone. You talk to Dr Patterson for a moment, Mrs Selby, and I'll go and see if I can find some more.' He stood up, walked round the desk and strolled from the room.

As the door closed behind him Kirstin glanced at the patient and saw that she was staring down at her hands.

'There really isn't anything to worry about, you know,' she said quietly. 'Hysterectomy is a very straightforward procedure these days.'

'It's not so much the op I'm worried about,' muttered Mrs Selby.

'So, what is it?' Kirstin leaned forward slightly.

The woman looked up then and eyed Kirstin as if summing her up.

'It's all right,' Kirstin said gently. 'I am a doctor, you know.'

'So's Dr Hardiman,' said Mrs Selby darkly, 'but he's a man and, I don't care what anyone says, they don't understand the same. How can they? Stands to reason, don't it?'

'So how about trying me?' asked Kirstin and, as the woman glanced nervously over her shoulder at the closed door, went on quickly, 'You say it's not the operation itself?'

'No.' Mrs Selby shook her head, hesitated, then said, 'It's more what happens afterwards.'

'What do you mean, "afterwards"?' Kirstin frowned.

'Well, me mum had the op,' Mrs Selby said at last. 'You know, it was all taken away—before she was forty—same as me, and she swore it brought on her change—hot flushes she had, one after another, and moody, well, you never saw nothing like it. I thought she were going to kill my brother once. Then, after that. . .'

Mrs Selby appeared well into her stride now, Kirstin thought.

'. . .after that, she went funny—you know, in the head. She wouldn't go anywhere; she couldn't remember anything, and she thought everyone was talking about her. Terrible it was; nearly drove my old dad round the bend, and she swore it was all because of the op. Me dad thought so as well. He said she was fine before she had it done.'

Mrs Selby paused for breath then, leaning across the desk and not giving Kirstin a chance to comment, she said, 'I couldn't cope with all that, Doctor. I've got me job to think about, and now that our Tiffany's marriage has broken up she's come back home to live with her two kids. I just can't afford to be acting strange—not now.'

Kirstin took a deep breath. 'I think, Mrs Selby,' she said firmly, 'you'll find that times have changed since your mother's hysterectomy.'

'Women are still the same—life's still the same,' said Mrs Selby with sudden, disarming insight, 'and I dare say the operation is still the same.'

'Yes,' agreed Kirstin, 'you're absolutely right. But one thing that has changed is the advances that have been made in modern medicine and in some of the attitudes and techniques applied to the operation itself.

'Let me explain,' Kirstin went on when she realised that the blank expression was back on Mrs Selby's face. 'When your mother had her hysterectomy,' she continued when she knew that she had the other woman's attention again, 'I dare say that not only did she have her womb removed but her ovaries as well. Is that so?'

'Goodness knows.' Mrs Selby shrugged. 'Haven't got a clue. What difference does it make?'

'Quite a lot, actually,' replied Kirstin. 'You see, even

after the menopause—the change—a woman's ovaries go on producing tiny amounts of a hormone called oestrogen. Now this hormone is vital for many reasons and without it women can experience all kinds of very unpleasant symptoms.'

'Like my mum did?'

'Exactly.' Kirstin nodded. 'So these days, if it is at all possible, when he is performing a hysterectomy the surgeon will try, if he can, to save the ovaries, or at least one of them. . .'

'What if he can't?'

'I was coming to that,' said Kirstin. 'If, for any reason, he can't—say, for example, if the ovaries were diseased—then following the operation the patient is given regular doses of oestrogen to replace what she will be missing.'

'Really?' Mrs Selby looked up quickly but still seemed doubtful. 'Does it work?'

'Yes, it has excellent results,' replied Kirstin. 'Not only does it help with the symptoms you described your mother having, but research has shown that it safeguards against a very distressing condition called oesteoporosis—or thinning of the bones—and in some cases against heart disease.'

'Does it mean lots of injections?' Mrs Selby was looking suspicious again. 'I can't stand injections.'

'No,' Kirstin replied, 'HRT can be given by mouth in tablet form, or as tiny patches or even as an implant—'

'HRT!' Mrs Selby looked shocked.

'Yes, that's what I said,' Kirstin replied. 'That's what it's called—'

'But that's dangerous; I've read in the paper; there were these letters—these women wrote in and said it's dangerous.'

'Were there any letters from women who had taken it and found that it worked?'

'Well, yes,' admitted Mrs Selby, 'but. . .'

'Do you know what the letters HRT stand for?' asked Kirstin, and when the woman shook her head, she said, 'Hormone Replacement Therapy. It's as simple as that. No mystery about it. It simply replaces the hormones that have stopped being produced, either by the loss of ovaries or because the ovaries have ceased to function.'

'So, if I go ahead and have this operation maybe life won't be so bad as I thought? Is that what you're saying?'

'I think you will find that life will be a whole lot better than you ever thought it could be.' Kirstin smiled. 'What symptoms were you having to make Dr Hardiman send you to Mr Blaine in the first place?'

'Bad periods.' said Mrs Selby quickly.

'Painful, you mean?'

'Oh, yes, and heavy. Flooding—you know what I mean?'

Kirstin nodded. 'Well, just think. There will be an end to all that. I expect you were getting tired, too, weren't you?'

Mrs Selby nodded and would doubtless have gone into further detail but at that moment the door was pushed open and Charles Hardiman came back into the room. In his hand was a bundle of leaflets, one of which he handed to Mrs Selby. 'Sorry to have kept you waiting,' he said. 'I got waylaid in Reception—it always happens as soon as I put my nose outside this door—but that's the leaflet I was telling you about. I think you'll find it will cover any questions you may have about your operation.'

'Thanks, Doctor.' Mrs Selby stood up. 'I'll take it, but I doubt I'll need it now.'

'Oh? And why is that?' Charles had retreated behind his desk again but he paused and looked over his glasses at his patient.

'Dr Patterson has explained it all to me,' said Mrs

Selby and then, as she reached the door, she paused and looked back, her gaze flickering from Charles to Kirstin then back to Charles again. 'I don't feel so bad about it all now.'

With that she went, closing the door behind her— leaving Charles with a look of astonishment on his face and Kirstin feeling rather uncomfortable.

'What in the world did you say to her?' asked Charles, sitting down heavily.

'Nothing much, really,' mumbled Kirstin, trying to busy herself with with the bundle of leaflets which Charles had dumped on the desk and which she now picked up and began slotting into a wire rack.

'Well, you must have said something. When I went out of the room she seemed on the point of refusing surgery; when I come back she positively skipped out of the room as if she hadn't a care in the world. So, come on, what was it? What did you say?'

Kirstin shrugged. 'I only explained the merits of HRT to her, that's all.'

'You mean she wasn't aware of them?' Charles looked vaguely surprised.

'Apparently not. Oh, she'd heard of it, of course, but appeared to be under the impression that it was still very much in the experimental stage. She also seemed terrified that she would suffer the same fate as her mother who experienced quite horrific reactions following her own hysterectomy many years ago. I hope I was able to reassure her and explain what is available today.'

Charles stared at her and for one awful moment Kirstin thought that she had overstepped the mark but, to her relief, he said, 'Well done, Kirstin. Obviously all that was needed was someone who would listen, then explain. I think we as GPs become so bogged down sometimes that we fail to realise that.'

'From what I've seen so far I would say the main

problem is not that you get bogged down by situations,'
said Kirstin. 'I would say it's simply that there isn't
enough time.'

'But if only we could find the time to explain and
to educate people more it would ultimately lessen our
workload.' Charles sighed, took off his glasses and began
to polish them. 'I must say, though, you seemed to have
survived your first week at Maybury very well.'

'Thank you.' Kirstin smiled. 'I must admit I've
enjoyed it, even though I've been out of my depth more
times than I care to say.'

'That's inevitable to start with,' Charles replied.

'I think it's been more with the people themselves than
with the medical situations,' replied Kirstin. 'And I don't
only mean the patients,' she added darkly. As soon as
she'd said it she wished she hadn't.

'You mean the staff?' Charles raised his eyebrows
and when Kirstin shrugged but refrained from further
comment he pressed the point even more. 'Has anyone
been giving you aggravation, Kirstin? Because, if so, I—'

'No, Charles, no,' she said hastily. 'It's not that; really,
it's not. It's just the unfamiliarity of the place and the
fact that, as you know, everyone has their own way of
doing things. Really, I shall get used to everyone's ways
in time—the same, I hope, as they will get used to mine.'
She gave a light laugh in an attempt, she hoped, to close
the subject.

'Well,' said Charles dubiously, 'if you're sure.'

'Quite sure,' she replied firmly.

'In that case,' said Charles, 'as Mrs Selby was the last
one, at least for the time being, I suggest you go and
find yourself some coffee.'

As Kirstin made her way to the staffroom she wondered what Charles would have said if she had told him
that, yes, she was finding the attitude of certain members
of staff difficult to understand.

She didn't, for example, think she would ever get onto
the same wave length as Eva Sansome, who seemed to
run the reception on similar lines to a concentration camp.
At the same time, Val Metcalf had not been the same
towards her since the unfortunate incident on her first
day when the nurse had thought Kirstin had gone over
her head to Dr Brolin.

And, predictably, he—Harry Brolin—had been the
worst offender of all.

Kirstin sighed then, as she reached the staffroom, she
pushed open the door. Mercifully the room was empty.
She poured herself a coffee and took the mug to a chair
by the window where she sat down and, curling her hands
around the mug for comfort, sipped the hot liquid.

She had made a determined effort to avoid Harry
Brolin as much as possible during that first week, and
most of the time she had been successful. On the few
inevitable occasions they had been forced into each
other's company Kirstin, each time, had reached the con-
clusion that her first impressions of him had been
correct—that he was arrogant and self-opinionated.

She sighed again and stared out of the window at the
main road and the relentless stream of traffic. Her gaze
roamed from the row of derelict houses, dwarfed by an
old gasometer directly opposite the centre, to the groups
of youths loitering on the street corners. Rubbish over-
flowed from the waste bins on every lamp-post, and a
supermarket carrier tossed by the chill March wind blew
along the dirty pavements. In a moment of rare indul-
gence Kirstin allowed her thoughts to turn towards home.

Even before she'd left the Island had almost been ready
for another summer season. By now boats would be in
the water after their winter hibernation and soon the
Solent would come alive in a blaze of coloured spinnakers
and white sails. The gardens of the Bembridge house
would already be a riot of spring colour; the daffodils

would be out and the lilac and mimosa in bud.

She glanced at her watch. Almost eleven o'clock. Her mother would probably just have come indoors after exercising the two family Labradors at the Duver. . . It seemed a lifetime away. . .years ago since she too had walked the dogs on the beach. . .she and Scott. Scott would be thousands of miles away by now in New Zealand. Was he missing her? Was he, too, missing the Island?

She blinked and swallowed. Was this—what she was feeling—a case of homesickness? If she hadn't known better she could have been excused for thinking it might be.

'Nothing to do?'

So lost had Kirstin become in her thoughts that she hadn't heard anyone come into the room. Looking round so sharply that she slopped coffee over her hand, she saw to her dismay that it was Harry Brolin and that he was also helping himself to coffee.

'What do you mean—nothing to do?' Shocked from the burn of the hot coffee on her fingers, she spoke more sharply than she might have done.

Harry shrugged. 'Just thought it's early for you to be finished, that's all.'

'I could say the same about you.'

'Ah, but I haven't finished yet. I'm merely taking a breather.' He took a mouthful of coffee and crossed to the large bookcase that dominated one wall, scanning the shelves before selecting a reference folder.

'So, how has it been?' he said at last, turning to Kirstin again with the folder under one arm.

'How has what been?'

'Your first week.'

'Oh, that.' She tried to remain cool but was irritated to find that, as always in his company, she felt on edge. 'It hasn't been too bad.'

'Good.' He turned to the door, taking his mug of coffee with him. Kirstin was relieved that he didn't intend to stay.

'Oh, one other thing,' he said as he reached the door.

Kirstin's heart sank.

'Are you still looking for a flat?'

'Not exactly. . . I. . .'

'You mean you've found somewhere?'

'No. . .'

'In that case, I thought you might be interested—a studio flat has just become empty in the block where I have my apartment. I understand the studios aren't very big but, for a comparatively short period of time, I would think it would be ideal. . .and if, as you say, you haven't found anywhere yet.'

Kirstin took a deep breath. 'No,' she said at last, 'I haven't, but that is because I haven't yet started looking. Charles and Estelle have impressed on me that there is no hurry.'

'True,' he said, 'but no doubt you'll be wanting your own place as soon as possible. After all, one can't impose for ever.'

She stared at him in angry silence. How dared he suggest that she was imposing on the Hardimans? They had made it perfectly plain that she was welcome to stay with them for as long as she liked. Certainly until she found somewhere suitable.

And that, thought Kirstin as Harry Brolin left the staff-room, definitely wouldn't include an apartment in the same premises as his.

Two days later Estelle and Charles arranged a supper party at their home for the partners by way of a welcome to Kirstin.

The gesture was kindness itself but for some reason Kirstin found the gratitude she should have felt swamped by a feeling of dread as the evening approached. She wasn't entirely sure of the reason for this but suspected that it might have something to do with the fact that because Bruce Courtney's wife, Sue, had been invited, along with Rhannie's husband, Sanjay, that left only Harry Brolin and herself who were unattached.

The thought of being paired with him, even if only temporarily for the evening, irritated Kirstin beyond reason. She decided that Harry Brolin himself couldn't be too enthralled by the prospect either, if his manner towards her had been anything to go by.

On the other hand, she thought as she soaked in the bath on the evening of the party—wondering what she should wear—maybe he was bringing a partner with him.

He wasn't married, she knew, but that didn't mean that he didn't have a girlfriend, or a fiancée even or, come to that, a live-in lover who shared that apartment with him.

For some reason the thought made her suddenly shiver. What sort of woman would Harry Brolin choose? He had made it quite plain that he didn't like her, so did that mean that he didn't like her type; that he wasn't attracted by tall slim brunettes?

Miss Rich Girl, he'd called her in a disparaging way. Did that mean that he also despised money and all it implied?

What would her opposite be? Kirstin mused. A waif-like, blue-eyed blonde? Someone like Hayley in Reception, perhaps? Hayley had certainly found Harry Brolin attractive, in spite of the difference in their ages, yet somehow Kirstin couldn't imagine the two of them together, and as she stood up and stepped out of the bath she found herself smiling at the idea.

Maybe, she thought, he would bring Hayley with him tonight, if only to prove her wrong.

She dressed with great care in an expensive jacket and

trousers in a soft scarlet material cut on loose, flowing lines, added simple gold jewellery and a generous spray of her favourite French perfume. On going downstairs, she found herself peeking into the dining-room to see how many places were set for supper.

When she saw that there were, in fact, just eight she didn't know whether she was dismayed or relieved.

'Kirstin, my dear, you look lovely.' Estelle, in an emerald-green two piece that set off her ash-blonde hair to perfection, met her in the hallway. 'That scarlet suits your colouring so well. Tell me, is there Latin blood in your family?'

'My grandmother's family came from Cornwall and have a host of stories about Spanish sailors and Cornish maidens.' Kirstin laughed.

'How romantic,' murmured Estelle. 'Isabella Fedora is Spanish, you know.'

Kirstin nodded. 'Yes, we've already compared notes and, I must say, we hit it off straight away.'

'I'm afraid she isn't coming tonight,' Estelle said as she led the way into the drawing-room, where Charles was waiting for them. 'We've kept the guest list to partners and spouses. Once you start inviting other members of staff it's difficult to know where to draw the line without offending anyone.'

'I can imagine,' replied Kirstin, smiling at Charles as he stood up to greet them.

After pouring drinks, Charles proposed a toast to a pleasant evening and a little later the doorbell rang.

The Bannergees were the first to arrive—a glowing Rhannie, exquisite in a peacock-blue sari trimmed with gold braid, and her husband, Sanjay, a rather intense young man who seemed to lack his wife's serenity.

They were closely followed by Bruce Courtney and his wife, Sue, a volatile redhead who liked to dominate the conversation and who seemed to provide the apparent explanation for Bruce's permanent state of anxiety.

Harry, predictably, was the last to arrive and as Estelle led him into the drawing-room Kirstin, who had been watching the door, found that his gaze seemed automatically drawn to hers. It was in that instant as he looked at her that she saw something in his eyes, some emotion or reaction she'd never seen there before.

If she hadn't known better she would have said that it was admiration or, at the very least, pleasure at seeing her.

But that was ridiculous. This was Harry Brolin. And it was her, Kirstin Patterson, that he was looking at.

It was Sue Courtney who, as they moved into supper, asked the inevitable question. 'Who's on call tonight?'

'I have that dubious pleasure.' It was Harry who replied. 'I wonder if I'll get beyond the main course.'

'The last party we attended Bruce didn't even get through the starter,' retorted Sue.

'I don't even attempt to go out when I am on call,' said Rhannie as they took their seats.

'Neither do I usually,' said Harry, 'but Estelle made it quite plain that this was a special occasion. She said she wanted us all present so it was inevitable that one of us would be on call.' He smiled at Estelle.

'It is a special occasion.' It was Charles who replied. 'It seemed only fitting that we should welcome Kirstin in a proper fashion.'

'And how could I miss that?' Harry gave a slight nod, his eyes again meeting Kirstin's as he took his place directly opposite her at the dining-table.

If there was mocking sarcasm in his tone only she appeared to detect it for the others all nodded and murmured in enthusiastic agreement.

The conversation around the table as the wine flowed and one delicious course followed another centred mainly on practice talk, turning at last to the topic of night visits.

'I do not allow Rhannie to go alone,' said Sanjay. 'It is no longer safe. Whenever she gets a call during the evening or at night I accompany her.'

'I think you're very wise.' Bruce looked more melancholy than ever. 'I must admit I tend to take the dog in the car with me if I'm called out at night.'

Some good-natured laughter followed about who would be the most effective in a dangerous situation—Sanjay or Bruce's dog.

'Have you done any night visits yet, Kirstin?' asked Sue.

Kirstin shook her head. 'No, I must confess I haven't. Charles hasn't woken me when he's had night calls.'

'Going easy on her to start with, eh, Charles?' asked Harry, sipping the tonic water he'd been drinking all evening.

'Something like that.' Charles smiled then added, 'There's plenty of time for all that.'

'Mustn't frighten her too much or she'll be hightailing it back to the Isle of Wight.'

Harry's eyes met hers yet again and quickly Kirstin looked away, recalling how he'd predicted that she would last no longer than a month at Maybury.

Mention of the Isle of Wight was the cue for the conversation to change as first Rhannie, then Bruce, asked Kirstin questions about her home and her lifestyle.

Apart from two phone calls requesting advice, Harry did not receive a call-out until the party was almost on the point of breaking up.

'Could be a police job,' said Bruce as Harry disappeared into the hall to answer his pager.

'Police job?' Kirstin looked up quickly, wondering what he meant.

Bruce nodded. 'Yes, Harry does a lot of work for the police; didn't you know?'

When Kirstin shook her head Charles said, 'Sorry,

Kirstin, I should have told you; I forgot.'

'What exactly does he do?' she asked curiously.

'Well, if someone is taken into the police station and has been injured or is taken ill while in custody that's when Harry is called in. Likewise, if a body is found he would be called in to certify the death.'

'Sounds interesting,' said Kirstin slowly.

'Wouldn't be my cup of tea,' muttered Bruce, looking up as Harry suddenly appeared in the doorway again.

'I have to go over to the Parkside Estate,' he said, glancing round at everyone.

'Rather you than me,' said Bruce.

'The police are there—some sort of domestic dispute that's got out of hand, by the sound of it. Anyway, I have to go. I'm sorry, Estelle.'

'That's all right, Harry,' Estelle replied. 'We were just telling Kirstin about your police work—she didn't know about it.'

'Is that so?' Again his eyes met hers.

'Yes,' she replied lightly. 'I was just saying that it sounds interesting.'

'It is,' he turned to go. 'Tough, but interesting.' He paused. 'Want to come along?'

Kirstin stared at him.

'I don't know about that. . .' Charles began uncertainly.

Harry smiled. 'No, on second thoughts, maybe not. Not really in your line, I wouldn't think. . .'

There was probably something about the way he said it, some implication that prompted her response.

'I'd love to come.' Her reply was cool and in the silence that followed even Kirstin herself couldn't believe she'd said it.

Harry's gaze didn't waver. 'Change out of that outfit,' he said, 'and get a warm coat—I shall leave in precisely two minutes.'

As Kirstin hurried from the room she heard Charles, in a worried voice, say, 'I really don't know about this, Harry.'

'The experience will be good for her, Charles.' She heard Harry's reply, then no more as the door closed behind her.

CHAPTER FOUR

WHAT in the world had prompted her to agree to come with him? Kirstin thought as she sat beside Harry Brolin in the big Citroën and they hurtled through the night to the Parkside Estate. He hadn't said a word since they'd got into the car and Kirstin herself had hardly dared to speak. Now, as they sped through the deserted streets, it crossed her mind that he would be stopped for speeding if he wasn't careful.

And as they approached a roundabout on the outskirts of Maybury it seemed that her fears were about to be realised as a police car appeared from nowhere, flashed its lights and began chasing them.

Kirstin froze and then, as Harry Brolin barely slowed down, she dared a sidelong glance. Only his profile was visible in the darkened car, silhouetted against a backdrop of streetlights. Kirstin had already thought that it looked as if at some time in the past his nose had been broken and although that irregularity showed up now it was impossible to see his expression.

It came as quite a shock therefore when she heard a low chuckle. She stared at him in astonishment.

'Don't you think you should stop?' she said, and was furious that her voice came out on a squeaky high.

'Stop?' He flung her a surprised glance. 'Whatever for? This is an emergency.'

'I know. . .but. . .the police. . .'

'What about the police?'

'Well, they are chasing us, in case you hadn't noticed!'

'Chasing us!' He sounded incredulous.

'Yes.' Kirstin glanced over her shoulder. 'Since that last roundabout, to be exact—'

'They're not chasing us!' He laughed again.

'They're not?' she said weakly.

'No. They're escorting us.'

'Escorting. . .? Oh!' Suddenly she felt silly. She should have known. But, on the other hand, how could she?

'How did they know?' she asked after a moment. 'Who you were, I mean.'

'This car is pretty well known,' he said. 'Apart from which, I dare say the message that we've been called out was picked up by the patrol cars.'

Kirstin fell silent and slid down a little further in her seat, then quite unexpectedly she felt a sudden surge of adrenalin. This certainly seemed more exciting that sitting in surgery.

'Do you know what it's about?' she asked as they left the dual carriageway and entered what seemed like a labyrinth of darkened streets.

'I don't know a lot,' he replied. 'Simply that it's a domestic dispute. There's been some violence and the police requested my presence. . .'

He offered no further attempt at speculation, remaining silent until—after what seemed like travelling for miles into the very heart of the labyrinth—he leaned forward slightly and peered through the windscreen.

'Ah,' he muttered, more to himself than to Kirstin, 'this looks like the place. . .'

Ahead Kirstin could see the blue flashing lights of another patrol car, parked by the side of the road. Groups of people were congregated in the road, their faces ghostly in the strange glow from the yellow streetlights.

Harry pulled up behind the police car, and the second patrol car stopped behind them. A uniformed officer from the first car walked back to them and Harry wound his window down.

'Dr Brolin.' The officer nodded and, bending forward, looked at Kirstin.

'Hello, Mel,' said Harry, 'this is Dr Patterson.'

Kirstin suddenly felt absurdly pleased that he had actually acknowledged the fact that she was a doctor. She certainly hadn't expected him to. Then she felt angry with herself for being pleased. Why shouldn't he acknowledge the fact, for heaven's sake? After all, she was a doctor.

'What's the situation?' Harry was speaking to the officer and Kirstin forced herself to concentrate.

'Looks like we could have a hostage situation developing.'

'Do we know the story?'

'Not entirely, but it seems like a domestic situation between a young woman and her boyfriend who live a few streets away. As the result of some violence between them, the woman came to this address. . .' the officer turned and glanced at the house behind him '. . .where we believe her family live.

'The man apparently followed her,' he went on as Harry and Kirstin listened, 'and more violence took place, involving, we think, the woman's father and her brother. There are also small children in the house, although it isn't clear who they belong to.'

'Do we know the nature of any injuries?' asked Harry

'There's been at least one stabbing, possibly more. It is more than likely that both the boyfriend and the brother were armed with knives. The woman has a head injury; oh, yes, and her brother has a history of severe mental problems. It seems the brother has locked himself in a bedroom with the children to stop the boyfriend getting to them. We have actually detained a man we believe to be the woman's boyfriend.'

'I see,' said Harry, his voice grim. 'Have Social Services been informed?'

The officer nodded. 'Yes, in view of the nature of the brother's past history, it seemed advisable. An ambulance has also apparently been called by a neighbour and is on its way from Maybury City General.'

'Right, well, we'd better see what we can do.' Harry wound up his window and opened his car door.

'What about me?' asked Kirstin.

He glanced over his shoulder. 'You have two options.' His voice sounded completely matter-of-fact as if, to him, the knives and the stabbings were an everyday occurrence. 'You either sit here in the car or you come with me.'

Kirstin swallowed. 'I'll come with you,' she said.

'Right,' Harry said as she joined him on the pavement. 'You stay close, and you do exactly as I tell you. Is that clear?'

She nodded. 'Yes.'

'Good. Let's go.'

Together with the police officer they made their way along the pavement. As they passed the police car Kirstin caught sight of a man, his shaven head covered with tattoos, sitting in the rear seat with another officer beside him.

The crowd, mostly of women gathered round the gate, fell back as they approached the house which was ablaze with lights.

A third officer met them at the front door. He looked very young, and his face was ashen. Without a word he led them into the house, down a narrow hallway and into a small sitting-room. A man, lying on the floor, was bleeding heavily from a stab wound to his stomach. A youngish woman was slumped against an armchair. Her nose was bleeding profusely.

An older woman who appeared on the point of hysteria was ineffectually darting between the two of them.

The remains of a meal of pie and chips was on the

table and in one corner Trevor McDonald was reading *News At Ten* on the television.

Harry crossed the room and turned off the television, apparently assessing the situation as he did so, then he knelt beside the injured man, opened his case and took out a couple of pairs of latex gloves and a packet of gauze pads.

'Put these on—' he handed one pair of gloves to Kirstin '—and take some of these pads and see if you can help there.' He nodded towards the young woman.

Kirstin did as he said and, crouching beside the woman, handed her one of the gauze pads. It was pretty obvious that the woman's nose was broken and she had also lost a front tooth.

'It's all right,' Kirstin reassured her. 'Pinch the bridge of your nose—look, like this.' She demonstrated. 'That should help to stop the bleeding. The ambulance will be here soon to take you to Casualty,' she added as she helped to mop up the blood.

'I'm not going anywhere till I know the kids are all right,' said the woman through gritted teeth.

'Tommy won't hurt them,' gasped the older woman, who by this time was kneeling on the floor beside her husband while Harry was doing his best to staunch the flow of blood from the injured man's stomach.

'So why's he got them in the bedroom?' shrieked the young woman.

'To stop that maniac you lived with getting his hands on them,' yelled her mother.

'Ron is not a maniac—it's Tommy who's the maniac. They should never have let him out of that hospital in the first place.'

'You've changed your tune, Linda,' shouted her mother. 'It was a different story when Ron chased you round here, wasn't it? Couldn't get out of his way fast enough then, could you? Still, it's your own fault for

living with him. I always said you should have stayed
with Dave. . .I knew this one'd be trouble. You've only
gotta look at him.'

The woman turned to Kirstin. 'I always said something
like this would happen.'

'How many children do you have?' asked Kirstin, turning to the young woman again.

'Three,' replied Linda, dabbing cautiously at her nose.

'And they are all upstairs?'

The older woman nodded. 'Yes, Linda moved in here
with them two days ago when he—her fancy man—
turned violent after drinking himself stupid. She went
back to get her things from his place this evening. They
had a fight and he chased her back here—' She broke
off as a low groan came from her husband. 'Oh, God!
Bert,' she gasped. 'Is he going to be all right?'

'He's lost a lot of blood,' said Harry. 'Give me a hand
here, Kirstin, to set up a drip.' She worked with Harry,
securing the saline drip with difficulty in the
confined space.

They had only just finished when the paramedics
arrived. They administered oxygen to the injured man
and while they were transferring him from the floor to
a stretcher the police officer who had spoken to them
outside the house came into the sitting-room and looked
at Harry.

'Dr Brolin,' he said, 'do you think you could try to
persuade Tommy to unlock the bedroom door?'

'I want to get this man settled first,' replied Harry
shortly then, glancing up at Kirstin, he said, 'You
have a go.'

'Me?' For one moment she was startled.

'Why not?' Harry raised one eyebrow. 'Do you have
a problem with that?'

'No, no, of course not,' she replied hastily. 'I'll see
what I can do.' Scrambling to her feet, she carefully

stepped over Linda's legs and joined the officer at the door.

'I'll come with you.' Linda attempted to get up but the effort proved too much for her and with a groan she slumped back against the settee.

'No.' Harry was emphatic. 'Leave it to us. Besides, Linda, you'll need to go to Casualty.'

'I'm not going anywhere till I know my kids are safe,' she said again.

Kirstin hurried from the room and had just began to climb the stairs behind the officer when a voice from below made her stop and look back.

Harry was standing in the hall with one hand on the newel post as he looked up the stairs.

'Yes?' she said, her eyes meeting his.

'Be careful,' he said. 'He has a knife, don't forget.'

Kirstin felt her heart give a sudden lurch but whether from fear or because of the expression in Harry's eyes—one which she was at a total loss to understand—she didn't know. It was almost as if for a moment he was genuinely concerned about her.

But that was highly unlikely. He was probably wondering how he would explain it to Charles if she got herself attacked.

'Of course,' she replied, and was amazed at how casual her voice sounded.

When she reached the landing she found the officer trying the door-handle of a room at the back of the house. He turned and shook his head at Kirstin.

She moved behind the officer and listened.

There was only silence from inside the room and then she heard a faint sound, a sound which at first she was unable to identify but which suddenly with a certainty that chilled her blood she realised was the sound of a child whimpering.

'Come on, Tommy,' called the officer, turning the

handle again, 'it's time you came out, you know.'

There was no answer and the officer shrugged help-lessly and turned to Kirstin.

'You see?' he said and when she nodded he added, in a very low voice. 'We don't want to break the door in unless we have to because if we frighten him there's no telling what he might do to the children.'

'Isn't he supposed to be protecting them?' whispered Kirstin and when the officer nodded she went on, 'Surely he won't hurt them? He's their uncle, isn't he?'

'Yes, but he also has a long history of mental problems, and he is armed. We simply can't take any chances— listen, you have a go at trying to talk to him. He may respond to you.'

The officer moved away from the door and Kirstin, taking his place, listened again. The whimpering had stopped.

She took a deep breath, then in a low voice she called, 'Tommy.'

There was no reply.

She tried again with the same result, then she tried a little louder. 'Tommy, will you talk to me?'

Again silence followed but this time, after the silence, a faint sound was heard from inside, as if someone had moved to the door.

'Tommy, are the children all right?' Kirstin asked.

Another silence.

'Tommy,' she began again but this time, unexpectedly, she was interrupted by a voice from the other side of the door.

'Jill? Is that you, Jill?'

Kirstin glanced at the officer.

'Who's Jill?' she mouthed, but the man shrugged again and shook his head.

'No, Tommy.' Kirstin turned back to the door. 'It's

not Jill. My name is Kirstin. I am a doctor, and I want to help you.'

There was another long silence then a noise that sounded like a sob, but whether from Tommy or from one of the children they had no way of knowing.

Then Tommy spoke again.

'Where's me mam?' he said.

'She's all right, Tommy,' Kirstin replied. 'I expect she'll be going to the hospital with your dad in the ambulance.'

All was quiet again and Kirstin was just wondering whether she should try another, quite different approach when Tommy spoke again.

'It weren't me, you know, what did it. It were him.'

'Did what, Tommy?'

'Knifed me dad. I were trying to get the knife off him. . .but they'll say it was me. They always do. . .' he added. Even through the closed door there was no mistaking the bitter helplessness in his voice.

'You do have the knife, Tommy, don't you?' said Kirstin.

'Yeah. I got it off him in the end after he started on our Linda.'

'Don't you think it might be a good idea to give me the knife now, Tommy?'

'Why?'

'Well,' replied Kirstin carefully, knowing that every word she said could be crucial and that anything might tip the balance, 'you said yourself they blame everything on you. If you haven't got the knife they won't be able to put any more blame on you, will they?'

'There was another silence and then, doubtfully, Tommy said, 'What about the kids?'

'Linda's waiting for them.' Kirstin found herself holding her breath, willing him to open the door, but a moment later her hopes were dashed.

'I'm not opening the door with that psycho down-stairs—he's a raving loonie.'

'Who do you mean, Tommy?' asked Kirstin, knowing full well who he meant but needing him to say so himself.

'That Ronnie Sykes, of course. Who the hell did you think I meant?'

'He's not there, Tommy. . .'

'He'd just as likely knife the kids—he's like that. He'd do it just to get back at our Linda for leaving him.'

'I told you, Tommy, he isn't there.'

'What d'you mean, he isn't there? Course he's there, he knifed me dad, didn't he? When the old man tried to stop him getting to Linda he stuck his knife into him, just like he was a pig or summat.'

'I tell you, Tommy,' said Kirstin patiently, 'he isn't there now. The police have him. When I arrived I saw him in the back of a police car.'

There followed another long silence while Kirstin and the officer waited in an agony of suspense.

'How do I know you ain't lying?' At last Tommy spoke again.

'I promise you, I'm telling the truth,' said Kirstin, and in growing desperation she went on, 'Listen, Tommy, I told you, I'm a doctor. Do you really think I'd let those children anywhere near a man like that? They would be so frightened.

'In fact. . .' she paused'. . .they must be frightened now seeing that you have a knife. . . Don't you think we should let them see their mum?'

'Kayleigh and Simon are asleep. . .'

'That's good, but the other one. . .?'

'Stephen?'

'Yes, Stephen; didn't I hear him crying?'

'Yeah,' Tommy replied. 'Stephen got a bit upset. Wanted his mam.'

'So don't you think it would be a good idea to let him see his mum, Tommy?'

There was yet another long silence before the unmistakable sound of muffled sobbing started again.

'I think we're going to have to break the door down,' muttered the officer. 'It's going on too long. . .'

'Let me try just once more,' said Kirstin. Vaguely she was aware that Harry had come up the stairs and was standing on the landing behind her and the officer, but in that moment her only concern was for the human drama being played out around her.

'All right.' The officer nodded. 'Just once more, then. . .'

But Kirstin didn't wait to hear what he was going to say; instead, she turned back to the closed door.

'Tommy,' she said urgently, 'do you remember when you were in hospital?'

Silence.

'Do you remember how you felt. . .?'

'Jill was there. . .' he said falteringly.

'Yes,' Kirstin agreed, desperately wishing that she knew who Jill was, then—taking a gamble—she went on, 'You had Jill, but didn't you miss your mum?'

Silence. 'Yeah, I did miss her. . .'

'Then you know how Stephen must be feeling now. He is missing his mum too. He wants to be with her, Tommy. Will you let him go to her?'

There was another long silence and just as Kirstin was thinking that she had failed,' there came the sound of the key being turned in the lock, followed by the rattle of the doorhandle.

'Let's have the knife, Tommy,' said the officer urgently as the door was cautiously opened a few inches. 'Throw it out.'

The door opened a little more but instead of the knife being thrown out onto the ground it was handed out, and

because Kirstin was standing directly outside the door—
between Tommy and the officer—it was she who took it.

In the brief moment before she handed it on to the
officer she was only too aware of the vicious looking
object in her hand, with its ridged bone handle and long,
serrated-edged blade.

She shuddered involuntarily as the officer took it from
her and, turning back to the room, she braced herself as
to what she might be about to see.

But as she prepared to enter the bedroom she felt a
restraining hand on her arm and, turning, she found it
was Harry who was holding her back as a second officer
and a WPC raced up the stairs and onto the landing.

'Well done,' Harry murmured, 'but it's police in first.'

Only seconds later a dishevelled-looking young man,
presumably Tommy, was hustled from the room by two
of the officers. As he passed Kirstin he threw her a
wild-eyed look.

In that moment she felt quite desperate; felt that she
wanted to speak to him, to say something—anything—
to reassure him in some way. But it was not to be for at
that moment the WPC appeared in the bedroom doorway
and looked questioningly at Harry.

'Come on, we can go in now,' he said.

With one last backward glance at Tommy as he was
bundled down the stairs, Kirstin followed Harry into the
bedroom.

All three children were in one double bed. Two were
asleep but the third, a little boy, no more than four years
old with his hair a tangle of blond curls, was sitting on
a pillow, his eyes wide with fright and tears running
down his cheeks.

'Stephen.' Kirstin sat on the bed beside him and gently
smoothed his hair out of his eyes. 'Are you all right?'

The child nodded then, at the sound of a sudden commotion outside, he turned his head towards the door.

Linda rushed into the room just as one of the other children, a girl, awoke and started crying. She grabbed both children, fiercely hugging them to her.

Stephen, looking over his mother's shoulder at Kirstin, said, 'I want Tommy. Where's Tommy gone?'

'I don't think we're required here any longer.' Harry touched Kirstin's arm and she stood up.

Leaving Linda with her children, she followed Harry downstairs where they found that the WPC had just opened the front door to admit a young, fair-haired woman.

'Hello.' The woman looked tired but had a lovely smile. 'I'm Tommy's social worker,' she said. 'My name is Jill Meadows.'

'What will happen to him?' Kirstin threw Harry an anxious glance as half an hour later they travelled back through rain-washed streets to the Hardimans' house.

'Tommy? Oh, nothing much. I expect they'll review his case again.'

'Shouldn't he be in hospital?'

'Probably. He was once, then he was released into care in the community.'

'Do you agree with that?' She threw him a curious glance.

'Sometimes, yes.' He nodded. 'Too many people have been locked away in the past for too long and for no good reason.'

'But surely when there is a danger. . .?'

'There are too many like Tommy.'

Kirstin fell silent for a moment and, recalling the look on Tommy's face when he had passed her on the landing, she said, 'Would he have harmed those children, do you think?'

'I doubt it.' Harry hesitated, then shrugged. 'But who knows? He may have harmed them and truly believed he was protecting them from a greater evil.'

'He seemed to be close to Jill Meadows.'

'He is. Tommy loves her. She is probably one of the few people he feels he can trust. Your voice must have reminded him of Jill. You did well there, by the way.'

'Thank you.' Suddenly Kirstin felt ridiculously pleased.

They were silent then as they sped back through the night.

'It's late,' said Kirstin, peering at her watch as they drew up in front of the house. 'I expect they will have gone to bed.'

'They've left a light burning for you.' Harry nodded towards the front door, where a light could be seen shining through the glass fanlight.

'Yes.' She paused not knowing quite what else to say.

'That was a bit of a baptism of fire tonight,' said Harry unexpectedly. 'It's not always like that, you know.'

'No, I didn't imagine it would be.'

She fell silent again and suddenly she became very aware of him as he sat beside her in the darkness. She really felt that she should say something else but she couldn't think what. She could hardly thank him for a nice time.

In the end it was Harry who spoke.

'Don't you think you'd better get to bed?' he said. 'Maybe you're not tired after all that excitement but I am, and if we don't get some sleep soon the mob will be howling at the door for surgery before we know where we are.'

He'd done it again, she thought angrily. Made her feel stupid. With a muttered apology she got out of the car and, before closing the door, she mumbled something about seeing him the next day.

'You go on in,' he said. 'Charles would never forgive me if I didn't see you safely inside the premises.'

She nodded. 'Yes, all right. Well, goodnight, then. . . Harry.'

'Goodnight.'

She hurried away from him up the path, unlocked the front door and let herself into the lighted hall. He didn't drive away until she'd closed the door.

With a sigh she leaned against the door. It had been quite a night. She would be the first to admit that and, yes, now she came to think about it she supposed that she was tired.

But before she had simply felt exhilarated; while she had been with Harry Brolin her adrenalin had flowed. Not that it could have been anything to do with him, of course; it had simply been the nature of the circumstances that had made her feel so charged up.

After all, she told herself as she made her way up the stairs to bed, it wasn't every day that a girl found herself responsible for disarming a man with a dangerous weapon.

It wasn't until she was actually in bed that Kirstin realised just how tired she was, and almost immediately she fell into a deep sleep.

She was awoken barely an hour later by Estelle, shaking her shoulder.

A white-faced, distraught Estelle who told her that Charles had collapsed.

CHAPTER FIVE

CHARLES was lying on the floor in the open doorway of the bedroom.

'He got out of bed and said he wanted the bathroom,' said Estelle as Kirstin knelt beside him and searched for a pulse. 'He seemed to fumble around, then he fell. Oh, he isn't dead, is he? Please, God, not that.'

'No, he isn't dead,' said Kirstin, checking that his airway was clear, 'he's unconscious. Help me here, please, Estelle; that's right, open the door further while I move him.'

Carefully she manoeuvred Charles onto his side and into the recovery position.

'What is it?' Estelle sounded frantic. 'What's happened to him?'

'I would say he's had a stroke.' said Kirstin, scrambling to her feet. 'I'll just get my case.'

Leaving the near-distraught Estelle crouching beside her husband, she hurried back along the landing to her bedroom where she collected her medical case.

On her return she again checked Charles's pulse then, taking her stethoscope from her case, she gently moved him again and listened to his heatbeat. She rolled up the sleeve of his pyjama jacket and checked his blood pressure.

'We need to get him into hospital,' she said, glancing up at Estelle. 'Stay with him while I go and phone for an ambulance.'

She phoned from the bedroom and when she spoke to Ambulance Control she was asked if she'd called a doctor.

'I am a doctor,' replied Kirstin. 'I am attached to the Maybury City Practice.'

'I understood Dr Brolin was on call for that practice tonight.' The ambulance controller sounded suspicious.

'He is,' replied Kirstin swiftly, 'but, as I've just said, I am also with the practice and the patient happens to be the senior partner—Charles Hardiman.'

'Good Lord, Doctor Hardiman?' The man sounded astonished. 'Why didn't you say?'

For one moment Kirstin thought he was going to ask what she was doing with Charles Hardiman in the middle of the night, but he didn't. Instead, he assured her, that he would have an ambulance with her in a very short time.

'They're on their way,' Kirstin said to Estelle on her return to the bedroom. 'They shouldn't be too long.'

'Do you think we should call Harry?' asked Estelle anxiously. Her face looked pinched and drawn and she appeared to have aged at least ten years since the previous evening's dinner party.

'I can't see that's necessary,' said Kirstin. 'He would only do what I have done.'

'Yes, I suppose so. . . It's just that Harry is our GP.'

'Is he?' Kirstin was aware of a sense of surprise. She wasn't sure why because it stood to reason that the Hardimans would be registered with someone. The surprise was that it should be with Harry rather than Bruce who, after all, was the next in seniority to Charles.

Then came the agony of waiting for the ambulance to arrive.

Kirstin checked Charles's pulse and heatbeat several more times, noting as she did so that the right side of his face seemed twisted.

Estelle spent the time alternating between kneeling on the floor beside her husband and pacing up and down to the bedroom window to look for the headlights of the awaited vehicle.

At Kirstin's suggestion she and Estelle took it in turns to throw on some clothes and when the paramedics at last arrived they accompanied Charles and the crew to the waiting ambulance.

'He seems fairly stable,' said Kirstin to one of the paramedics, 'so I'll take my car and follow you, then I'll be able to bring Mrs Hardiman home later.'

The paramedic nodded but as he closed the ambulance doors he gave Kirstin a curious glance.

'I don't think we've met, have we?' he asked.

Kirstin shook her head and wondered what he had been told by Ambulance Control. 'No, I don't believe we have; I'm Kirstin Patterson—Doctor Patterson.'

'Pleased to meet you, Doc. No doubt we'll be seeing quite a bit more of you in the future.' He nodded and hurried round to the driver's seat, leaving Kirstin to get into her own car which was parked on the Hardimans' drive beside Charles's Volvo.

For the second time that night Kirstin found herself driving through the deserted streets of Maybury. But this time she was alone and her escort was an ambulance instead of a police car.

They seemed to reach Maybury City General Hospital in a very short space of time and Kirstin followed the ambulance into the parking bay of the accident and emergency unit.

She explained to the duty staff who she was and what had happened to Charles then, as he was whisked away to an emergency treatment room, she bought hot tea for herself and Estelle from a vending machine in the reception area.

'Thank you.' Estelle took the plastic cup and, as she put her hands round it for warmth, Kirstin noticed that she was shaking. 'I must let Juliet know,' she said suddenly. 'She will want to be here.'

'How far away does she live?' asked Kirstin.

'Fifty miles.'

'Would you like me to phone for you?'

'No.' Estelle shook her head. 'I must do it myself.' She only drank half the tea then went off to the payphone, leaving Kirstin to drink her own tea.

When she returned Kirstin looked up anxiously. 'Did you speak to Juliet?' she asked.

Estelle nodded. 'Yes, she's on her way here.'

'Good.' Kirstin drained her cup.

'I also phoned Harry,' Estelle said.

'Harry?' Kirstin looked up quickly. 'Why?'

'I told you. He's our GP.'

'Yes, I know, but he can't do any more, and now that Charles is here—'

'I know, Kirstin, I know.' Estelle looked exhausted. 'Please don't think I'm not grateful for what you did— for the fact that you were there—but I know that Harry would want to be told.'

'True, but I thought it could probably wait until morning.' Kirstin shrugged.

'What you have to understand,' said Estelle, and suddenly her voice sounded firm as if she had somehow gained control once more, 'is that Harry is not only Charles's GP but his partner and, even more than that, he is his friend. He would want to be told because if anything should happen to Charles he would want to be here.'

'Oh,' said Kirstin suddenly subdued. 'Oh, I see.'

They were mostly silent after that, then Kirstin went to the loo where she splashed her face with cold water to fight off the lethargy that was threatening to get the better of her.

When she came out her heart gave an uncomfortable lurch as she saw that Estelle was talking to Harry Brolin.

He barely acknowledged Kirstin as she approached, just a slight inclination of his head, and before she had time to say anything he said, 'I'll go and see what I can find out.'

He disappeared through swing doors at the end of Reception, as dynamic and energy-charged as ever—in spite of the fact that it was three in the morning and he'd had little or no sleep that night.

Kirstin sank down again onto the hard wooden chair beside Estelle. They sat in silence amidst the bustle of the busy casualty unit for what seemed like eternity but which, in actual fact, could not have been more than half an hour at the most.

It was the sight of Harry, coming back through the swing doors in animated conversation with a white-coated doctor, that stimulated them both into action again.

Estelle stood up as the two men approached and anxiously scanned their faces, her gaze finally coming to rest on Harry's granite-like features.

'Harry. . .?' The single word held all her fears for her husband.

'He's all right, Estelle, for the time being, at least,' Harry replied gently. 'I've been in to see him. He's suffered a CVA—a stroke that has affected his right side.'

'Will he be paralysed?' Estelle's voice wavered slightly.

'Possibly. Probably.' Harry pulled no punches. 'He's still unconscious.'

'Can I see him?'

Harry glanced at the white-coated doctor. 'Mahmood?' he said.

The man nodded. 'Of course,' he murmured. 'Shortly we will move him up to the ward. If you would like to come with me, Mrs Hardiman.'

Kirstin watched, her heart aching for Estelle as she followed the doctor through the swing doors.

'I do hope he'll be all right—but I did notice it was

his right side that was affected so that could mean his speech may be impaired—' She turned as she spoke, only to be interrupted by Harry.

'Don't,' he said, and his voice was like the crack of a pistol, 'don't ever do anything like that again.'

'What do you mean?' Kirstin stared at him in astonishment.

'Exactly what I say. If you value your future as a GP don't ever dare to go over my head again.'

'But I wasn't. . .I mean I didn't. I don't understand. . .'

Harry didn't reply and Kirstin felt a sudden swift surge of anger. 'So what should I have done?' she demanded.

'You should have called me,' he replied tightly.

She stared at him. Speechless.

'Are you saying I shouldn't have called an ambulance?' she managed to say at last. 'That I shouldn't have got him to hospital?'

'I'm not saying anything of the sort,' Harry retorted. 'What I am saying is that you should have called me.'

'But I didn't even know Charles was your patient until Estelle said—'

'So you did know that?'

'Yes, but—'

'That makes it even worse,' he snapped.

'Right.' She was really angry now. Her cheeks had grown hot as she faced Harry across the hospital reception. 'So, tell me, what should I have done? Left him on the floor to die while I tried to contact you?'

'Don't be ridiculous.' He glanced over his shoulder as if suddenly aware of where they were and of the one or two interested looks they were getting from the patients waiting for treatment.

Lowering his voice he said, 'All I'm saying is that you should have contacted me. I was the duty doctor, and you knew I was. Even if you'd done it after you'd called the ambulance.'

'Oh, so that's what this is about, is it? The fact that it was you on duty and not me? That you think I might be usurping your position? I should have known.' She gave a short, derisive laugh.

'Will you keep your voice down, Kirstin?' he muttered with another glance over his shoulder. 'We don't want details of this all over Maybury. I am simply making the point that as duty doctor I should have been informed as to what was happening.'

'I didn't feel it was necessary,' she replied, controlling her voice with difficulty. 'You could have only just got to bed after the other incident and I was quite capable of coping with a CVA. You seem to have forgotten I am fully qualified—'

'I haven't forgotten anything of the sort.' His voice was quiet now, but somehow more deadly than when it had been raised. 'I am sure you coped and administered first aid admirably, but it doesn't alter the facts. I was on call. You knew I was duty doctor, and Charles is my patient. You say your motives were entirely charitable, in not dragging me out of bed, but I wonder—was it that, Kirstin, or were you trying to exert your authority? Prove how good you are by ignoring the procedures?'

'Of course not,' she muttered, avoiding his gaze which was making her feel decidedly uncomfortable. 'I just didn't think. . .'

'Ah, you didn't think. Now we're getting somewhere. There was nothing charitable about your actions at all, was there?' Taking her arm, he moved her none too gently through the entrance doors and into the relatively quiet foyer where they couldn't be overheard.

'You weren't really bothered how many times I'd been called out,' he said softly. 'It simply didn't occur to you that I should be informed, did it?'

'I was more concerned with the patient,' Kirstin replied coldly, at the same time thinking how correct her first impressions of this man had been. Just for the briefest of times there, when she had accompanied him earlier that night, she had wondered if she might have been mistaken; if she had misjudged him; that he wasn't as bad as she had first thought.

Now she knew that her instincts had been right—that he really was overbearing and self-opinionated.

'And, as far as I'm concerned,' she went on rapidly, 'I not only did all that was required of me, but I did it correctly.'

'Right. So what did you do? Tell me.'

'What—now?' she protested, glancing back into Reception then outside into the still dark grounds of the hospital.

'Why not?' He shrugged. 'Neither of us is going anywhere until Estelle comes back.' As he spoke he motioned her towards a bench-type seat inside the main doors and they both sat down.

Kirstin took a deep breath and then, thinking—not for the first time—how unusual, menacing even, his tawny-coloured eyes were, she began to recount what she had done from the moment Estelle had called her and she'd found Charles lying on the floor. When she had finished Harry didn't speak; just sat there, gazing at the tiled floor.

'So, did I do right or not?' she demanded at last.

'What?' he looked up, frowning, and Kirstin found herself wondering if he had actually heard a word she'd been saying. At the same time it suddenly struck her how tired and worried he looked.

'With Charles. Did I do right?' she repeated.

'Yes,' he said wearily, 'of course you did.'

She breathed a sigh of relief and was about to ask him what all the fuss had been about when he said, 'It's no more than I would have expected. You are qualified, after all.'

'So why. . .?'

'But you still need to learn there is far more to being a GP than textbook techniques.'

She was about to retort that she agreed and that surely initiative played its part somewhere but something stopped her, whether it was the sudden wave of weariness that assailed her or the slump of Harry's shoulders as he leaned forward and covered his face with his hands she wasn't sure.

Whatever it was, she remained silent and when she recalled Estelle saying that Charles was not only Harry's patient and partner but that he was also his friend she was glad she had.

'Do you think he'll be all right?' she asked at last in a small voice.

'Depends what you mean by all right.' Harry lowered his hands. 'If you mean will he live the answer is that we won't know for the next few days, which could be crucial, but if you mean in terms of disability if he does live then your guess is as good as mine. . .'

He trailed off as a car suddenly drew up at the entrance and a woman got out of the passenger seat. She said something to the driver, before slamming the door and striding to the entrance.

In spite of the hour she looked casually elegant, with a loose camel coat thrown over a tan velour catsuit and with her blonde hair drawn back from her face and secured at her nape with a black bow.

And as she swept through the glass doors the woman's resemblance to Estelle left Kirstin in no doubt that this was her daughter, Juliet.

Harry stood up to greet her as she walked towards him, her face anxious, her eyes seeking his.

'Harry. . .?' was all she said.

Kirstin glanced at him and was amazed to see an expression on his features that she'd never seen before.

A softer expression. Almost one of tenderness, if he were capable of such a thing.

'Juliet.' He opened his arms and she walked straight into his embrace.

'Is he. . .? Oh, he's not. . .?'

'No. He's all right,' Harry murmured gently against the soft, ash-blonde hair. Your mother is with him at the moment. Are you alone?' He glanced at the door.

'No, Paul brought me. . .'

'Ah.'

To Kirstin, watching, the scene was charged with emotion—more emotion even than would be expected, given Charles's condition—and she found herself wondering about Juliet. . .and about Harry.

But there was no time for further speculation because Estelle appeared at that moment and more emotional greetings followed.

'Harry, you go home.' Estelle paused, before getting back into the lift again. 'And you, Kirstin,' she said. 'Thank you. Thank you both for everything. We shall stay for a while.'

Then they were gone, back up to the ward to be with Charles, leaving Harry and Kirstin alone again.

'I suppose we'd better do as she says and salvage what little there is of the night,' said Harry. 'Before we know where we are it'll be time for surgery and, believe me, it won't be easy—not with one short.'

'Don't forget me,' said Kirstin quickly as they left the main hospital building and began walking towards their cars. 'I can take a surgery. Charles had already let me take a couple on my own.'

'So you're suggesting you replace him now, are you?' His voice was heavy with sarcasm.

'No. No, of course not.' She felt her face grow hot again and was glad of the cover of darkness that hid it from his cynical gaze. 'I merely thought I could be a help in the situation.'

'You need supervision,' he replied shortly. 'You could be more of a liability than a help. We'll need a locum. But we'll discuss it later. Go home and get some rest.'

Whether his voice softened slightly Kirstin couldn't be sure but, if it had, the result didn't come anywhere close to how it had been when he'd greeted Juliet.

'See you later.' He was gone, leaving Kirstin to get into her own car while wondering anew just what the relationship was, or once had been, between Harry Brolin and Juliet.

That there was something was without doubt, for in that moment Kirstin had seen a side to Harry Brolin she'd never seen before. A side she would never have thought existed.

She didn't sleep during what was left of the night, spending the time instead wondering what would happen to her. It seemed pretty obvious that Charles would be out of action for some considerable time, that was if he ever would be able to return to work which—given his age and the severity of the stroke—seemed unlikely.

This, of course, would leave Kirstin without a trainer.

The more she thought about it the more probable it seemed that she would have to return home and the process would start all over again to find somewhere for her to do her trainee year.

This fear was reinforced later that morning when Bruce faced the rest of the Maybury staff during an emergency meeting and explained the situation.

'Harry is trying to arrange for a temporary locum to cover for Charles, at least for the time being, until we know what is going to happen,' he said, looking round at them all. 'In the meantime, I'm afraid we will have to muddle through as best we can. Rhannie, Harry and

myself will divide Charles's list between us. . .so I suggest, if no one has any questions, we make a start.' He
glanced at his watch then looked up quickly as Kirstin
suddenly spoke.

'I have a question,' she said, and everyone looked
at her.

'Ah, yes, Kirstin.' Bruce stared at her as if until that
moment he had forgotten her existence.

'What do you want me to do?' she said.

'Well, now, let's see. . .' Clearly Bruce didn't know
what to say. In the end it was Isabella who spoke.

'Couldn't Kirstin simply take over Charles's surgery?'
she said. 'It seems the obvious solution in the circumstances.'

'I don't think so.' Predictably it was Harry who
answered. 'Maybe, just for the moment, Isabella, she
could give you and Val a hand in the treatment rooms?'

Isabella glanced at Val, who shrugged in her offhand
sort of way.

Kirstin was just on the point of saying that maybe it
would be better if she simply went home and got out of
everyone's way when the intercom sounded.

Harry, who was the closest, answered it then pulled a
face as he replaced the receiver. 'It's pandemonium in
Reception,' he said curtly. 'We'd better get started. It's
going to be one hell of a day.'

'Just a minute.' Isabella held up her hand. 'What about
Dr Hardiman? Has anyone organised anything?
Flowers?'

'I dare say Eva will do so,' replied Harry and, glancing
at Kirstin, he added, 'On the other hand, maybe that's
something you could do.'

She had to bite back an angry retort. Was that all he
thought her capable of—organising a collection? Quite
obviously it was, just as it was obvious that he was still
angry with her for last night.

She watched helplessly as the staff prepared to go.

'There is just one other thing,' Harry said curtly. 'Rhannie, Bruce, could I have a quick word before we start?' The rest of the staff filed out of the room, leaving the three partners together.

'You come with us, Kirstin,' said Isabella. 'We'll find plenty for you to do.' It was plain that the nurse was trying to make her feel better but it did little to raise Kirstin's spirits.

Reception indeed resembled a scene from Bedlam as patients for early surgery jostled for seats, growing increasingly impatient with being forced to wait.

Kirstin found herself kept busy as she assisted the two nurses with dressings, blood tests, injections and other routine nursing procedures.

'What will happen now?' asked Isabella anxiously during a lull.

'What do you mean?' Kirstin frowned.

'Well, now that Dr Hardiman is sick—what will you do?'

'You won't be able to stay, will you?' Val turned from the store cupboard where she had been stacking supplies.

Kirstin thought she detected a note of satisfaction in her tone but she couldn't be sure, and decided to give her the benefit of the doubt.

'After all,' Val added, 'he was your trainer, wasn't he?'

'Yes,' Kirstin sighed. 'He was. I dare say I'll have to go home, and start looking for someone else to take me on.'

'That's a shame,' said Isabella. 'Just when you were getting settled in. . . But, who knows, maybe Dr Hardiman will be back?'

'I don't know about that. . .' Kirstin replied doubtfully. 'It was a severe CVA.'

'Did you see it happen?' Val suddenly seemed curious.

'Not exactly,' Kirstin replied. 'We had all been at a

dinner party given by Dr and Mrs Hardiman. . .'

'Dinner party?' Val frowned. 'We hadn't heard anything about that, had we, Isabella?'

'Oh, it was only the partners,' said Kirstin hurriedly. 'And their spouses,' she added.

'And you,' observed Val.

'Yes, and me,' agreed Kirstin lightly, 'and, really, I had to be there as Estelle—Mrs Hardiman—had arranged it by way of a welcome for me.'

'How kind,' said Isabella quickly, genuinely, while Val stared at Kirstin in apparent amazement.

'Was Harry Brolin at this party?' she asked stiffly.

'Yes,' replied Kirstin.

'But Harry hates parties.'

'Well, he was there. Until he got called out, that is.'

'So was that when Dr Hardiman had his stroke?' asked Isabella.

'No.' Kirstin shook her head. 'That was later, after I got back. I suppose I must have been in bed for about an hour when Mrs Hardiman called me and said that he had collapsed on the floor.'

'So where had you been?' asked Val suspiciously.

'Sorry?' Kirstin had turned away to clear soiled dressings from the trolley.

'You said, after you got back. Where had you been?'

'Oh, I went on the house call with Harry—Dr Brolin.'

'What?' Val stared at her.

'Yes.' Kirstin swallowed. 'It was interesting. It was a police call to a domestic disturbance.'

'Harry does a lot of police work,' said Isabella. 'If we want to track him down we always try the police station first,' she added with a laugh. At a sudden rap on the door she looked round. 'Come in,' she called.

The door opened and Eva stood there, hands on hips, glaring from one to another of them.

'Have you lot given up in here?' she demanded. 'In

case it's escaped your attention we have a near-riot situation on our hands out there.'

'Nothing you can't sort out, Eva, I'm sure,' said Isabella with a grin. 'But, no, we haven't given up. Send the next ones in.'

'Right.' Eva's eyes glinted dangerously behind her horn-rimmed spectacles but as she was about to turn away she appeared to remember something. 'Oh, one other thing,' she rapped, 'message from above. The partners want to see you, Kirstin, at lunchtime—in the staffroom.'

As the door clicked sharply behind Eva, Val turned to Kirstin and there was no mistaking the gleam in her eyes as she said, 'Sounds like that could be your marching orders, I would say, Kirstin. Wouldn't you?'

CHAPTER SIX

WHEN Kirstin went into the staffroom at twelve-thirty it was to find the partners already there, waiting for her.

'Kirstin, please come in and join us.'

It was Bruce, more anxious-looking than ever, who stood up and motioned for her to take a seat. Rhannie was sitting near the window and Harry, in an armchair in front of a low coffee-table, was furiously scribbling and didn't even look up.

Carefully ignoring him, Kirstin smiled at Rhannie, crossed the room, sat down and looked up at Bruce. 'You wanted to see me?' she said, and was surprised at how calm her voice sounded even to herself.

'Yes.' Bruce cleared his throat nervously. 'In view of what has happened, Kirstin,' he said, 'we have been discussing your position here. As I'm sure you will have realised, even if Charles is able to return to the practice—which I have to admit seems very unlikely the way things look at the moment—there is no telling just when that would be. It could be weeks, or it could be months. Or, like I said, it may not be at all.' He cleared his throat again and Kirstin wished he would stop waffling and get on with what he was trying to say.

'You, of course,' he went on, 'were scheduled to be with us—with Charles—for a year and I, that is, we. . .' Bruce glanced at his colleagues '. . .know that you must be eager to get on with your training so that you can take up your own position. However. . .' he paused '. . .with Charles out of action. . .'

'It's all right, Bruce.' Kirstin, unable to stand it any longer, interrupted him in mid-sentence. 'I realise the situation has created something of a problem for you, so I have already decided that I shall be returning home in the next day or so.'

There, she'd said it. Got in first. Saved Bruce the embarrassment of having to ask her to go. Out of the corner of her eye she was aware that Harry had stopped writing and was looking at her. She avoided his gaze, not wanting for one moment to give him the satisfaction of thinking that she might be upset at having to return home.

Suddenly she realised that Bruce was talking again, spluttering almost, and she forced herself to listen.

'. . .got it all wrong,' he was saying. 'Not what we meant at all.'

She frowned. 'I'm sorry,' she said. 'What exactly did you mean, Bruce?'

'We didn't mean for you to go home. . .' he went on.

'You didn't? But. . .' She stared at him in surprise.

'We meant for you to stay.' He glanced at Rhannie. 'Didn't we?'

'Oh, yes,' said Rhannie. 'We want you to stay.'

'But I don't see how I can.' Kirstin looked bewildered. 'Not without Charles here. He was my trainer. . .' She gazed up at Bruce again but the telephone on the table beside him had started to ring and he had turned to answer it.

'Yes,' he agreed with her as he lifted the receiver, 'but. . .' He held up one hand to silence her then trailed off as he listened to the person on the other end of the line.

Briefly Kirstin allowed her gaze to flicker first to Rhannie, who merely smiled—that mysterious smile of hers that gave nothing away—then even more quickly to Harry but he, no doubt utterly disinterested by the whole affair, had returned to his notes.

When at last Bruce replaced the receiver after finishing

his conversation he turned vaguely to Kirstin and when she raised her eyebrows questioningly he said, 'Ah, yes, Kirstin, now where were we?'

'We were talking about Charles being my trainer,' said Kirstin, with more patience than she was feeling.

'Ah, yes, well, it's a shame he can't continue with it,' said Bruce, 'but I'm sure you'll find the new arrangement will be satisfactory, and as we've already spoken to the General Medical Council and to your future partners and neither have any objections to the change of plan. . .'

'Change of plan. . .?' Kirstin was more bewildered than ever.

'Bruce.' It was Harry who, without even looking up from what he was doing, intervened. 'Don't you think it might be an idea to tell Kirstin exactly what that change of plan is?'

'What?' Bruce gazed from one to the other of them. 'Didn't I say?' he asked as Rhannie hid a smile behind one slim hand.

'No, Bruce, you didn't.' Harry was beginning to sound exasperated now.

'Well, I'm sure she'll be pleased. Won't you, Kirstin?' Bruce smiled and nodded at her. 'After all, it's very good of Harry—don't you agree?'

'I'm sorry, Bruce,' said Kirstin, 'you've lost me. What is very good of Harry?'

'Well, that he's agreed to take over, of course. Oh, didn't I say that?' He gazed owlishly round at them. 'How silly of me. You see, Kirstin, Harry has agreed to be your trainer.'

Just for a moment the room seemed to tilt crazily, and as it righted itself Kirstin heard Bruce say, 'So much better for you than having to go home and start all over again. A lot of time can be lost like that. Well, now that's all settled I really must get on with my house calls. Oh, we have a locum starting next week, by the way. We'll have to manage as best we can until then.' He stood up and as he left the room he was followed by Rhannie, leaving Kirstin alone with Harry.

She sat very still in shocked silence, hardly able to believe what had just happened. It seemed as if everything had been arranged over her head, with no one bothering to ask her what she wanted.

But if they had, what would she have said? She hadn't wanted to return home, it was true; to have to start from scratch again, looking for a new trainer, finding another practice and getting settled.

She should be grateful, she knew.

But Harry Brolin as her trainer?

It was like some sort of nightmare, and one from which there didn't seem to be any escape.

'I trust the new arrangement meets with your approval.' It was Harry who broke the silence, a silence which had grown into something almost tangible between them.

Kirstin swallowed. 'It would have been nice to have known what was going on,' she said at last.

'You mean you would have preferred to have been consulted?' He looked up and met her gaze and when she nodded in reply he said, 'We thought you would be pleased that everything was being sorted out and that we wanted you to stay here.'

'Well, yes, I am. Of course I am, but. . .'

'But what?' he said softly.

'I suppose I'm surprised.' She shrugged.

'Surprised by what?'

'That you should even consider taking on my training. When I first came here I got the impression that you wouldn't be interested in being a trainer. . . And since I've been here. . .well. . .'

'Well what?' Harry stared at her and Kirstin got the

distinct impression that he was finding some aspect of what she was saying amusing.

'Well, I would have thought,' she said, taking a deep breath, 'that even if you did want to consider training I would be the last person you would want to take on.'

'I'm not considering training as a permanent arrangement,' said Harry, pushing the set of records he'd been writing on back inside their envelope and standing up. 'The only reason I'm doing it is because of the situation and because it is what I know Charles would want and would expect of me.'

'Oh.' For one moment Kirstin didn't know what to say for he had just made it perfectly plain that he was only taking her on because he felt obliged to do so. He probably wasn't looking forward to it any more than she was.

'So,' he went on, in a firm, matter-of-fact voice, 'you will join me each day for surgery, and you will accompany me on any house calls I make.'

'When is this to start?' she asked, frowning.

'There's no time like the present,' he replied abruptly. 'You can do today's visits with me.'

'What about your police work?' she asked.

'What about it?' It was his turn to frown now.

'Well, what do I do if you are called out?'

'I can't see that there would be any objection if you were to accompany me. I'll check on it. Anything else you want to ask me?'

She hesitated, but only for a moment, then said, 'Yes, there is, actually.'

'Well, go on, then; what is it?' He was beginning to sound impatient now, as if he wanted to get on.

'Will I be able to take any surgeries on my own?'

'Not yet. No,' he replied bluntly.

'Charles was allowing me to,' she retorted.

'You had obviously convinced Charles that you were

ready to do so. I also shall need convincing before I'm ready to hand my patients over to you.'

She flushed. 'I assure you I am more than capable. . .'

'Good,' he replied lightly, 'then you shouldn't have too much of a job convincing me, should you?' He walked to the door. 'Now, we really must get on, otherwise it'll be time for afternoon surgery.

'Oh.' He paused and looked back to Kirstin, where she was still sitting in her chair and staring at him in dismay. 'There is just one other thing. I spoke to Charles's daughter, Juliet, on the phone just now. Charles has regained consciousness but he has suffered a degree of paralysis in his right arm and leg and on the right side of his face, and his speech is impaired.'

'Poor Charles,' said Kirstin, trying desperately to put her own worries to the back of her mind. 'It's what I feared. He'll need a lot of good nursing and physiotherapy.'

Harry nodded. 'I was coming to that. Juliet is moving in with her mother for the time being so that she is able to visit Charles more frequently, and she intends staying for a while after he is discharged from hospital to help with nursing.'

'In that case, I shall move out,' said Kirstin quickly. 'The last thing they want to contend with at the moment is a house guest.'

'I agree,' said Harry smoothly.

'I hadn't intended staying there for any length of time, anyway,' she said faintly, irritated by his manner.

'In that case, you might well reconsider my suggestion of the studio flat.'

Kirstin looked up sharply but before she could say more Harry continued in the same smooth tone, 'Not only would it solve your accommodation problem but it would also make sense for you to be in closer proximity to me for night calls.' He glanced at his watch.

'I'll meet you at the car in fifteen minutes.'

With a curt nod he was gone, leaving Kirstin staring at the closed door and reeling from all that had taken place since she had come into the room.

It seemed that not only was she expected to work alongside Harry Brolin in the future but that now she should live alongside him as well.

'I'm sorry but I won't be able to help you in here this afternoon.' Kirstin had gone straight from the staffroom to the treatment room and as she spoke she looked from Isabella to Val.

'Oh?' Isabella looked up while Val turned sharply from the examination couch, where she was changing the paper sheeting in preparation for a cervical smear clinic.

'Why not?' demanded Val. 'We could do with an extra pair of hands at this clinic.'

'Sorry, but I'm going out on house calls,' Kirstin replied.

'So you didn't get the sack, then?' Isabella smiled.

'Far from it.' Kirstin pulled a face. 'Looks like I'm going to be up to my eyes in it.'

'Who are you going out with?' Val's eyes narrowed suspiciously.

'Harry Brolin,' Kirstin answered.

'You mean, just temporarily, till you go home?'

'Actually, I'm not going home.' For some reason Kirstin felt an unexpected stab of pleasure at imparting that particular piece of information to Val.

'I say!' There was no mistaking the pleasure in Isabella's voice. 'Are they keeping you on?'

'Yes, the powers that be have decided I am to stay here.' Kirstin smiled.

'Well, I'm glad,' said Isabella, 'and you must be relieved.'

'Yes, I am,' said Kirstin. 'It would have been a real

bind to have to go home now and to start again from square one.'

'But who's going to be your trainer?' Val still had the same note of suspicion in her voice. 'Dr Hardiman was the only doctor here who was prepared to take on a trainee.'

'Well, they say there's a first time for everything,' said Kirstin, 'and this must be one of those times. Harry has agreed to take over my training.'

'Harry?' Val sounded incredulous at the prospect. 'For the whole year?'

Kirstin nodded. 'Seems so.' She shrugged. 'He's even said I can accompany him on police work.'

'He must have taken a real shine to you.' Isabella grinned. 'It's not often Harry Brolin takes to anyone like that, I can tell you. Isn't that so, Val?' She turned to her colleague but Val, tight-lipped, had turned away and before either of them could say more she stalked from the treatment room.

'Don't take any notice of her.' Isabella gave a sigh as she caught sight of Kirstin's expression.

'Does she have a problem where I am concerned?' Kirstin asked slowly, then added, 'or is it something to do with Harry Brolin?'

Isabella chuckled. 'I would say a bit of both.'

'They aren't an item, are they?' Kirstin asked, suddenly startled that she might have missed the obvious.

'Good God, no!' said Isabella. 'Although. . .' she paused '. . .that's not to say Val wouldn't like them to be. She's fancied Harry like mad for years now.'

'And Harry?' asked Kirstin quietly.

'No.' Isabella shook her head and, when Kirstin remained silent, added, 'Well, what do you think? Would you say Val is Harry's type?'

'No, I suppose not. . .' Kirstin said slowly at last.

Isabella chuckled again. 'Mind you, I'm not sure who

would be. . . And, let's face it, there can't be too many
women who would be prepared to put up with him. . . He
can be so, well, difficult at times—and that's being kind!'

A mental picture of Juliet, tall, cool, blonde Juliet,
flashed into Kirstin's mind and once again she recalled
the look on Harry's face when he had caught sight of
her and, indeed, the look on Juliet's face as she had
embraced Harry. And once again she wondered. . .

'Oh, no! Is that the time?' Isabella suddenly broke into
her thoughts. 'I must get on, Kirstin.'

'So must I,' said Kirstin, 'otherwise I will be sent
home—on the grounds of unpunctuality.'

He was already in his car by the time she'd collected her
case, put on her coat and hurried outside to the
compound.

He didn't speak as she opened the door and slipped
into the passenger seat beside him. In fact, he didn't
speak even after he had negotiated the busy Maybury
traffic and they were on the fringes of one of the vast
housing estates that seemed to surround the city centre.

Whether or not it was the same estate they had been
called to the previous night Kirstin had no way of knowing. To her they all seemed to look alike, with their tower
blocks, their maze of streets and the smaller units of
housing like endless, identical concrete cubes.

Today they had no escort but that did not seem to
deter Harry, who appeared to know exactly where he
was going.

'You know the area well,' said Kirstin as he negotiated
one narrow street after another.

'I should do,' he replied abruptly.

'I take it you've been here a long time?' She threw him
a curious glance as he stopped the car on the forecourt of
one of the high-rise blocks of flats.

'I was born here.' The reply was equally as abrupt as the last.

'Oh.' For some reason she was surprised. She waited, expecting him to elaborate—but he didn't.

Instead, he got out of the car and when she did likewise, he locked it. 'Let's hope it's in one piece when we get back,' he said, looking over his shoulder at two boys who were flinging stones at a line of Coke cans on the low wall around the forecourt. 'Shouldn't you be in school?' he shouted.

'Nah.' One of the boys looked up. 'We're ill, ain't we?'

'What's wrong with you?' asked Harry.

The second boy nudged his friend. 'He's one of the docs,' he muttered warningly.

The boys fled round the side of the building, and Harry sighed. 'Come on,' he said and Kirstin followed him through a set of reinforced steel doors into the entrance foyer.

'The lift's out of order,' Harry said. 'Are you up to the stairs?'

'I should hope so,' she replied indignantly. 'But how did you know about the lift? Should we report it?'

'Can if you like.' Harry shrugged. 'Not that anything would be done about it. It's been out of order for as long as I can remember.'

As they climbed the stairs they met a young woman, coming down with a baby in a buggy and two toddlers at her side.

'However does she manage with all these stairs?' Kirstin, aghast, was already beginning to pant.

'It'll be worse when she gets back,' said Harry. 'She'll have bags of shopping then and she'll have to drag the buggy up behind her.'

'How far are we going?'

'Top floor,' he replied cheerfully.

'How did I know you were going to say that?' Kirstin

was having to make a conscious effort not to let him see that she was out of breath.

At last they reached the top floor landing. It was a depressing place that seemed in another world, with its balconies, rows of tightly closed doors and lines of grubby washing.

'Who have we come to see?' asked Kirstin as they stopped before a dark green door, its paint chipped and peeling.

'A woman called Margaret Burns,' Harry replied, lifting his hand to knock.

'What's wrong with her?'

'Rheumatoid arthritis. She's almost totally incapacitated.'

'And she's living on the top floor of a tower block?' Kirstin stared at him incredulously.

'You've got it in one,' he replied softly as there came a shuffling sound on the other side of the door and a faltering voice enquired who was there.

'It's all right, Maggie. It's me.' He raised his voice. 'Harry Brolin.'

There came a muttered exclamation, followed by the sound of someone fumbling with a security chain, then—after what seemed like a very long time—the door was eased open a few inches and a woman peered out at them from beneath a cloud of wild grey hair.

'Can we come in, Maggie?' Harry asked.

'Who's she?' The woman screwed up her eyes and squinted at Kirstin.

'She's a doctor, Maggie. Her name is Patterson.'

With that the woman stood back and allowed them to enter the narrow hallway. Leaning heavily on elbow crutches, she closed the door, pushed past them and led the way into a small, cluttered living-room.

'How are you feeling today, Maggie?' asked Harry, slipping off his jacket and draping it over the back of a chair. It was almost unbearably hot and stuffy in the room, the heat coming from a two-bar electric fire.

'Bloody awful,' Maggie replied bluntly, lowering herself painfully into a chair.

'Your recent blood tests were an improvement on the last lot,' Harry said as he dragged a chair in front of her and sat astride it, resting his arms on the back, 'so that indicates to me that the new anti-inflammatory drugs we started are doing their job.'

'Huh! Ya could have fooled me,' replied Maggie bitterly. 'So what about me water works?—they ain't no better.'

'The MSU we took—'

'What's that?' Maggie interrupted. 'Why can't you lot speak plain English, then we might understand what you're on about?'

'Sorry.' Harry grinned and fleetingly it occurred to Kirstin, who had found herself watching him closely, how different he looked when he smiled. 'What I should have said was the sample of your wee that we tested showed that you have a water infection. Now, it could be a reaction to the new drugs but it could just as well be a bug you've picked up so, to be on the safe side, I'm going to give you a course of Septrin. You've had those before, haven't you, Maggie?' Leaning sideways, Harry drew her records out of his case and began to peruse her medication chart, but Maggie was faster.

'I've had enough to sink a battleship,' she said with a sniff then, after a glance in Kirstin's direction, she said, 'They sending you lot out in pairs now, same as the Old Bill?'

'No.' Harry, who had started writing out a prescription, laughed without looking up.

'Wouldn't blame them if they did,' Maggie went on. 'It's getting worse round here. Joe next door was broken into for the fourth time last week. . . So, what you up to, then?' She eyed Kirstin again, as if taking in every detail of her navy woollen coat and the bright patterned scarf she'd flung casually round her shoulders.

'Dr Patterson is just getting used to life as a GP, that's all.' It was Harry who replied.

'D'you like it, then?' said Maggie, still looking at Kirstin.

'I think I'm going to. . .' Kirstin replied, choosing her words with care. Harry didn't appear to be paying attention to what she was saying, but she had the impression that there wouldn't be much that escaped his notice.

Maggie, however, had no intention of leaving it there. She saw few people and her world had shrunk so much in the last few years that whenever she saw a chance for a little diversion she seized it.

'So, how do you get on with him?' She jerked her head in Harry's direction.

'Oh.' Taken aback by the directness of the question, Kirstin fumbled for an answer. 'Er, very well,' she replied.

'Really?' There was mischief in Maggie's dark eyes now and even the sallowness of her skin seemed to take on a sudden glow. 'He can be a miserable old devil at times,' she added wickedly.

'Is that so?' Kirstin struggled to keep her voice casual but she felt her lips twitch and had the sudden uncontrollable urge to laugh.

'Yeah, he needs a good woman,' Maggie went on. 'I've been telling him that for years—but will he listen?' She looked up at Harry. 'Heart of gold he's got under all that grumpiness—all it wants is for the right woman to find it.' She turned her attention to Kirstin again, as if assessing her suitability. 'Maybe you've got what it takes to—'

'Here's your prescription, Maggie.' Cutting her short, Harry handed her the form.

'How am I going to get that?' Maggie's voice took on a pleading, whine.

'Won't your Tracy be in later?' asked Harry briskly, standing up and putting on his jacket again.

'Yeah, but couldn't you just. . .?'

'Tracy will get it for you, Maggie.'

'Harry?' Kirstin began. 'Couldn't we. . .?'

But Harry was ushering her out of the living-room into the hall. 'We'll be away now, Maggie,' he called. 'I'll phone at the end of the week when you've taken the antibiotics and see how you are. Don't forget to put the chain back on the door after we've gone.'

'We could have got her prescription for her,' said Kirstin accusingly as they went back down the stairs, their footsteps echoing hollowly through the empty stairwell.

'No, we couldn't,' replied Harry curtly.

'Well, we could at least have dropped it into the pharmacy.'

'No.' He shook his head. 'Not even that.'

'Why not?' she demanded.

'Because we quite simply do not have the time.'

'Well, I don't think that exactly shows the caring side of our profession. It would hardly have taken a moment to stop at the chemist—'

'Maybe not,' he interrupted her. 'Not today, but what about next time?'

'What do you mean—next time?' She threw him a contemptuous glance as they reached the foyer and he opened the door and stood aside for her to precede him out of the building.

'Well, by then Maggie will have told everyone on the block that nice Doctor Brolin collects their prescriptions for them—'

'You're exaggerating,' Kirstin protested, but Harry

wasn't listening. His eyes were scanning the car for any signs of vandalism.

'Looks like someone up there is looking after us today,' he observed as he unlocked the car.

'I think it's dreadful that someone like Maggie should have to live in a place like this.' Kirstin looked up at the tower block before she got into the car.

'I agree,' said Harry.

'Something should be done about it.'

'Absolutely. What would you propose?' He threw her a quick glance as he switched on the engine and reversed across the forecourt.

'She should be rehoused—someone in her condition. The council should find more suitable accommodation. Why, that's the last place a woman with rheumatoid arthritis should be living—the top floor of a tower block.'

Lowering her head, and with a slight shudder, Kirstin gave a last backward glance at the tall concrete building. And as they drove away she noticed for the first time that several of the windows in the building were boarded up.

'Right,' observed Harry as they joined the traffic on the dual carriageway, 'so if you ruled the world you'd have Maggie rehoused?'

'Yes. . .'

'And what about the young woman we saw on the stairs with the three young children—would you rehouse her as well?'

'Well, yes,' Kirstin replied. 'You must agree it's hardly a suitable environment—'

'And Joe?'

'Joe?' She looked at him again but he was staring ahead, concentrating on his driving.

'Yes,' he said at last, 'Joe's the old boy who Maggie mentioned. The one who lives next door who's been burgled four times. Joe has lost his sight. Glaucoma. Should he be rehoused as well?'

When Kirstin remained silent he continued, 'And what about the Parkins family?' Not giving her a chance to answer, he went on, 'The Parkins have eight children; theirs is a three-bedroomed place—a bit bigger than Maggie's, I must admit, but hardly adequate for their needs. . . And then there's—'

'All right,' said Kirstin abruptly. 'There's no need to go on. You've made your point. There are a lot of Maggies and Joes but I still think that as GPs we should be able to do something; that what we recommend should carry some clout with the authorities.'

'I appreciate what you're saying,' said Harry after a while, 'and in an ideal world it would all make perfect sense. Unfortunately, what we live in is far from that, so we just have to get on and do the best we can for people.'

'And that doesn't include getting their prescriptions for them?' she asked coolly.

'You'll understand when you've been here a bit longer,' Harry replied.

Kirstin doubted it but somehow refrained from further comment. They made a number of other house calls before returning to the medical centre. After Harry had parked the car, she said, 'What have we got next?'

'Afternoon surgery,' he replied. 'Then. . .' he turned his head and looked thoughtfully at her '. . .I suggest you come and have a look at the studio flat.'

'Do I need to do that today?'

'It's unoccupied at the moment,' he replied firmly. 'You could lose it if you don't act fast.'

'So, where is it exactly?' she asked as she got out of the car.

'Down near the docks,' he replied.

Kirstin remembered that Estelle had told her that that was where Harry lived. Her heart sank as, with visions of the depressing tower block they had just left still fresh in her mind, she trailed into the building behind him.

CHAPTER SEVEN

It was almost dark when Kirstin and Harry arrived at the dockland site, and the block where Harry had his apartment appeared as little more than a black hulk among the skeletal outline of cranes against the skyline.

'It's an old warehouse,' said Harry as they walked towards the building, after parking their cars. 'And, just so there's no doubt, they even named it so.' He pointed to a brass plaque above the entrance lit by an old-fashioned coach lamp.

And any lingering comparison with the tower block they had visited earlier finally disappeared when they entered the building, walked through a stylish foyer with smart decor and entered the fully operational lift.

'We'll leave our cases in my apartment,' said Harry, 'then I'll see if we can obtain the keys to the studio flat.'

Kirstin was learning fast that her medical case could never be left in a car and, in spite of signs of extensive security, she had automatically brought it with her when she'd parked her car alongside Harry's in the private car park.

She was still very uneasy about living in such close proximity to Harry Brolin and at the same time was indignant that the matter seemed to have been taken out of her hands. But, in spite of these negative feelings, she could not help but be impressed when they stepped from the lift onto the third-floor landing and she was confronted by thick, comfortable carpets, a profusion of green plants—which she imagined to be artificial but which, on closer examination, proved to be real—and tastefully decorated walls with a selection of framed watercolour prints.

Harry produced a set of keys from his pocket and inserted one into the lock of an oak-panelled door. When the door swung open he preceded her into the room, switched on the lights and then closed the door behind them.

Kirstin looked around her, interested in spite of her resolve to remain indifferent to it all. The apartment was huge and open-plan, the two floors connected by an iron spiral staircase in one corner. The far wall looked as if it had retained the original brickwork and the high, arched windows of the warehouse while beyond, the myriad lights of Docklands twinkled in the darkness, merging with the stars above, their reflections shining in the silky blackness of the water.

'Oh!' said Kirstin. 'It's lovely. Quite lovely.'

'Yes,' Harry agreed, 'it is pretty impressive, isn't it?'

'Is the studio flat the same?' she asked quickly, eagerly.

'Not quite. It's on this floor but it's not so big, of course, and it doesn't have the same view.'

'Oh.'

He must have heard the disappointment in her voice for he said, 'But neither does it carry the same rent.'

'No. I suppose not.' She sighed. 'It was just that for one moment there I was reminded of home. I guess it was the water that did it, even though it's the river and not the sea.'

'Leave your case there—' he indicated a space beside a glass-topped coffee-table '—and we'll go and see about these keys, then you'll be able to judge for yourself what it's like.'

Ten minutes later, in possession of a second set of keys, Harry led the way to the rear of the building. As he opened the door Kirstin found herself waiting in anticipation.

It was, as he had explained, not so big—just the one floor, and that only about three-quarters the size of one of his floors and with no spiral staircase. But it was still spacious where it needed to be—in the main living area—and compact elsewhere, namely in the kitchen and bathroom. It had the same arched windows set into the original brick wall, but thick cream blinds were drawn down, shutting out the night.

Harry strolled to the windows and released one of the blinds. 'Like I said, you don't have the river view from here but it is pleasant. It overlooks the quay area, which has been restored, and the old towpath.'

The decor was in creams, beiges and browns with the occasional splash of scarlet which, for some reason, reminded Kirstin of poppies amidst cornfields and again evoked memories of home.

'What do you think?' Harry watched her as she wandered through the archway from the neat, efficient coolness of the kitchen to the living area with its vast, comfortable-looking sofa bed.

She had been more than prepared to say no—that it wasn't what she wanted at all; had, in fact, wanted to say that.

But how could she when it was exactly what she wanted?

'It'll suit me just fine,' she heard herself say, and all she could do in the end was hope that she didn't sound too eager.

'Good,' he said, 'I thought it would. Sorry about the view—not a lot I can do about that.'

'That's OK,' she replied lightly. 'You can't have everything.'

'I'll have a word in the appropriate quarter tomorrow,' he said, opening the main door again, 'then, I would imagine, you'd be able to move in right away.'

With a final, satisfied look round Kirstin joined him on the landing.

'I take it you have a sea view at home,' he said as he unlocked his own door and let them into his flat again.

'Yes.' Kirstin nodded, wondering why he shut the door behind them when they'd only come back to collect her case. 'Our house is near the harbour and looks out to sea.'

'Are you hungry?' he asked suddenly, abruptly changing the subject.

'Well, I. . .' she began, taken aback by the sudden switch of topic.

'You must be,' he said. 'It's been one hell of a day; you've had the same day as me, and I'm starving. What were you going to do?'

'I was going to go back to Estelle's. . .'

'Estelle will be at the hospital with Charles,' he said bluntly. 'Do you like pasta?'

'Yes,' she nodded, thinking that he was about to suggest they go to an Italian restaurant and wondering how she could refuse.

Instead he said, 'Take your coat off. I'll cook for us.'

He gave her no chance to refuse and, taking off his own coat and tossing it onto a chair, he crossed to the kitchen area—leaving Kirstin to her own devices.

Slowly she slipped off her coat, draping it round the back of another chair, then—involuntarily—she was drawn as if by a magnet to the windows and the night-time panorama beyond.

She wasn't sure how long she stood there, soaking up the almost magical atmosphere. That the magic would fade in the daylight reality of murky grey waters and unattractive container vessels she had little doubt but, for the moment, she was more than happy for that magic to create an impossible illusion.

Sensing Harry at her elbow, she turned sharply and

found that he had brought her a glass of red wine. Taking it from him, she said, 'How long have you been here?'

'In this area, you mean?'

'No, you've already told me you were born here. I meant this apartment.'

'I moved here when the warehouses and factory sites were first converted—about five years ago,' he said, adding, 'Must go; the pasta will burn.'

Sipping the wine, Kirstin turned back to the view.

The pasta, served in a thick herb sauce, was excellent and it wasn't until she began to eat that Kirstin realised just how hungry she was.

They ate in silence for a while then Harry spoke. 'I did have a particular reason for coming here to live,' he said, 'apart from the convenience and the obvious charm of the place.'

She paused, her fork halfway to her mouth, wondering what he was about to divulge.

'Many years ago,' he went on, 'when this was still a warehouse my father worked here, and his father before him. My father died when I was a boy. He had kidney disease. I felt that coming here to live forged a sort of link.'

'What about your mother? Is she still alive?' Suddenly Kirstin was interested. In spite of the tiredness which was slowly threatening to overtake her she wanted to know more.

'My mother died when I was born,' Harry replied briefly.

'So, who brought you up?'

'My brother and I were taken into care. We grew up in a children's home.'

She stared at him and suddenly so much seemed to fall into place—about his manner, his tough attitude and his sometimes seemingly jaundiced view of life.

'I would say,' he said, and as he spoke he allowed an unexpected smile to cross to features, 'that mine was a very different upbringing from yours.'

Kirstin nodded. 'You're absolutely right,' she agreed. 'Mine, I appreciate, was privileged. . . I was brought up within a close-knit, loving family circle—it couldn't, I suppose, have been more different, and yet. . .' she paused '. . .we've both chosen to follow the same profession.'

'True,' he agreed, 'although I suspect our paths were somewhat different.'

'Oh, I don't know,' Kirstin protested mildly. 'I would imagine the traumas of medical school and exams were the same, and I suspect the role of a junior houseman doesn't differ much. . .'

'Maybe not. But the life of a medical student would, I imagine, be eased if one was able to eat regularly, and the tiredness would, no doubt, seem less gruelling if one didn't also have to work endless hours in casual labour just to make ends meet.'

Kirstin drew a deep breath. It seemed that she was never to win where this man was concerned, and at this time of night it hardly seemed worth trying. 'Talking of tiredness,' she said trying to keep her tone light, 'after last night I'm almost dead on my feet. That was an excellent supper, Harry. But, if you don't mind, I think I really will have to be heading for home now.'

She stood up and paused as Harry's mobile phone rang.

She waited while he answered it, and when he said, 'I'll be right there,' she looked up sharply.

'I didn't think you were on call tonight,' she said as he replaced the aerial.

'I'm not,' he said. 'At least, not for the practice. That was the police. They want me to go down and examine a suspect who has been injured in a brawl.'

'Do you want me to go with you?' She stared at him, fighting her fatigue.

He seemed to consider for a moment then he shook his head. 'No,' he said and for once she thought she detected a note of compassion in his voice. 'No, you go home and get some sleep.'

'I really don't mind. . .' she began, not wanting to give him ammunition for thinking her a wimp and not up to the job, but at the same time knowing that all she really wanted to do was to sleep.

'I would prefer you to be on form for surgery tomorrow,' he said, abruptly cutting short any further discussion.

'Very well.' Quickly she picked up her coat and was still struggling into it as he grabbed his own jacket and opened the door.

They took the lift to the ground floor and just before the doors opened Kirstin looked at Harry and said, 'Thank you for supper, and for finding me somewhere to live.'

'You're welcome.' Briefly his eyes met hers—that unusual tawny gaze—and somewhere deep inside her she felt something stir. Maybe, just maybe, things might not be as bad as she had feared between them. Maybe they would get on after all.

The next moment, as the doors opened and they stepped out into the foyer her, hopes were dashed.

'It seems to me,' he said, 'we've been faced with a difficult situation but there's always a way round these things. We have no option but to make the best of a bad job. See you tomorrow,' he called over his shoulder as he walked to his car, leaving her to get into hers.

She sat very still for a moment as he drove away, and she watched the red tail lights of his car.

Was that how he saw her? A bad job? Something to be tolerated? If that was the case the prospect of the forthcoming year was pretty grim.

And yet, she thought as at last she switched on her engine and drove out of the car park, when they had been eating, when he had talked of his boyhood, she had seen yet another side to Harry Brolin—this time a vulnerable side. The side that showed a child up against all the odds. A child who had lost not only his mother but also later, and at a very early age, his father. A child, already born into a tough, uncompromising environment, who was raised in care. But, it would seem, a child who even then had ambition—an ambition that would take him through medical school to qualify as a doctor.

She'd likened him to a street fighter once and surely now that analogy summed him up better than any other.

The next few days were quite frantic as the partners struggled to cope with the extra workload until their locum arrived. For Kirstin the pressure was even greater as on the Sunday, far from having a day off, she moved out of the Hardimans' house.

'I feel quite dreadful about this,' said Estelle as she helped Kirstin to carry her belongings out to her car.

'Well, don't. . .' Kirstin, struggling under the weight of two large cardboard boxes, smiled at Estelle.

'But I do. It seems like we are hustling you out.'

'Not at all,' said Kirstin briskly. 'You mustn't feel that, really. And, besides, I would have found somewhere else eventually anyway.'

'I know. But that hardly seems the point.' Estelle shook her head. 'Heaven knows what Charles will say when he's with it enough to know what's going on.'

'I'm sure he won't mind,' Kirstin replied, slamming the boot shut with a sigh of relief. 'Especially when he knows that Harry has organised everything for me. He does seem to set great store by Harry's judgement.'

'Yes,' he does,' Estelle sighed. 'Yet it seems only

yesterday that the boot was on the other foot.'

'What do you mean?' Kirstin stared at her curiously.

'Oh, I'm talking about years ago when Harry first came to this house.'

'You mean when he first joined the practice?'

'Oh, no. Before then,' Estelle replied quickly. 'Long before then when Harry was at medical school and Juliet was doing her nursing training. . . Look, come and have a last coffee with me before you go and I'll tell you all about it. I don't have to be at the hospital for another hour.'

'I really ought to get on. . .' Kirstin glanced at her watch. It had been her intention to move her gear into her studio flat as quickly as possible, but she was suddenly intrigued by what Estelle was saying.

'Come on,' said Estelle, 'it'll help to stop me feeling so bad about you moving out.'

'In that case, how can I refuse?' Kirstin smiled and followed Estelle back into the house.

'You've got me intrigued,' she said a few minutes later as she watched Estelle set out china mugs and spoon ground coffee into the cafetière. 'About Harry, I mean. You say you've known him since his medical school days?'

'Yes, he was a raw young student in those days when Juliet first bought him home, but he was very sure of himself even then.' Estelle lifted the biscuit barrel down from the shelf. 'Shall we have a biscuit? I really shouldn't because I'm watching my weight, but I never could resist Hobnobs.

'Charles took to Harry straight away,' she went on, after Kirstin had taken a biscuit, 'I wasn't certain at first; he seemed a little too sure of himself for my liking, but I soon came to realise that he was only like that because he'd had to be. It's called survival, Kirstin, and, believe me, it's a jungle out there. It is today, and it was then.'

'And what about Juliet?' asked Kirstin quietly. Suddenly it seemed the most important thing in the world that she should know just where Juliet fitted in.

'Oh, she was smitten,' said Estelle, 'absolutely and utterly, right from the start. It was because he was so different, you see. Quite, quite different from the boys she had grown up with. They all came from comfortable, middle-class backgrounds, but Harry was different. He was a fighter; he was tough, and Juliet was attracted by that—at least, at first she was.'

'And Harry, what about him?'

'I rather think the same. Juliet was probably different for him. Vastly different from the girls he had known.'

'But he was attracted to her?'

'Oh, dear me, yes, very much so. In fact, I would go so far as to say he worshipped her. Having said that. . .' Estelle paused reflectively '. . .the romance wasn't without its stormy episodes, I can tell you. They split up several times before Harry came into the partnership, but they always seemed to get back together. They even became engaged. . .'

'So, what happened?' Kirstin stared at her, trying to picture the young, newly qualified Harry, starry-eyed and engaged to the senior partner's daughter and failing utterly to do so.

'Paul was what happened,' said Estelle. 'By then, you must understand, Harry had become almost like a son to us. Anyway, he—Harry, that is—went to Scotland on a course and while he was away Juliet met Paul at a hospital party. It was, if I remember rightly, to celebrate Paul becoming a registrar. And that was that.

'When Harry returned Juliet told him the engagement was off. . . I feared for Harry at the time,' said Estelle slowly. 'I'm sure it broke his heart and I really didn't think he was ever going to get over it. But, well, life goes on and one just has to come to terms with these things. . . But now, of course. . .' She broke off and glanced up sharply as a car came up the drive, its tyres crunching noisily on the gravel.

'Oh, here is Juliet now,' she said. 'We'd best change the subject, I think. I wouldn't want her to think we'd been talking about her. . .'

'No,' said Kirstin quickly, 'no, of course not.' But she'd heard enough. Enough to confirm what she'd already suspected. That at one time Juliet Hardiman, as she had been then, and Harry Brolin had been very close. Very close indeed.

She left soon after that and drove to the new apartment near the docks. It all looked very different in daylight, as she had thought it might, and even though the sun was shining, it was only a very pale watery sunlight and the river looked grey and rather murky.

Her flat, however, was warm and bright and she'd only been in the place for five minutes when she heard a tap on the outer door.

'Can I give you a hand with your gear?' Harry strolled through the open doorway. An off-duty Harry, looking more relaxed than Kirstin had ever seen him and younger somehow in a polo-necked sweatshirt and jeans.

'Thanks. I don't have that much. But it would probably seem like a lot after bringing it all up in the lift.'

They worked easily together, falling naturally into the pattern they had already established during the last few days when Kirstin had sat in on his surgeries and been by his side during every house call he'd made.

Today, however, she found herself looking at him in a new light in view of what Estelle had just told her.

'Where do you want this?' he asked, standing in the middle of the room with her mini stereo unit in his arms.

'Oh,' Kirstin looked round. 'Over there, I think. Yes, over there on that cupboard.'

'Interesting taste you have in music,' he remarked,

after plugging in the stereo and glancing quickly through her CD collection. 'Everything from Clapton to Puccini.'

'I have a lot more at home. I couldn't manage to bring them all with me. Do you like music?' she asked after a moment. Somehow, if he did, she couldn't imagine what his taste might be.

He nodded. 'Yes, jazz, mainly, and blues.'

She should have known. He would fit in perfectly in a smoky cellar with a saxophone wailing in the background.

'So, what else do you do on that island of yours?' he asked a little later when they'd carried everything in and it lay in a heap in the centre of the floor.

'Apart from listening to Clapton and Puccini, you mean?' she asked.

'I can't imagine you do that all the time.'

'No. . .' she paused, considering '. . .no, well, I like all water sports—swimming, windsurfing, water-skiing, oh, and sailing, of course.'

'Oh, of course,' he said.

She threw him a sharp glance, not certain whether he was mocking her or not. His expression was perfectly straight, however, so she still wasn't sure.

'I always have.' She felt compelled to defend herself. 'Pretty inevitable really, I suppose, with a marine business in the family.'

'So, what does it consist of—this marine business?' He leaned against the worktop in her tiny kitchen and folded his arms. He had pushed up the sleeves of his sweatshirt and Kirstin noticed the covering of dark hairs on his arms. She'd noticed it before on that first day when he'd dealt with the epileptic patient in Reception. For some reason, it had affected her then and it did so now. There was something intensely masculine about it, and she found herself hastily looking away.

'Boat-builders,' she said quickly. 'Yachts, mainly, and

chandlery. It was founded by my grandfather, but these days it is run by a limited company, managed by my father and his brother.'

'So do you, too, have brothers who will carry on this business?'

Kirstin shook her head and laughed. 'Afraid not. I'm an only child and my uncle has two girls who aren't interested, so it doesn't seem very likely somehow. My father lives in hopes that. . .' She trailed off, suddenly— for some reason she was at a loss to explain—not wanting to pursue that particular story.

Harry, however, seemed keen to know more. 'Yes,' he said with interest, 'what does your father hope?'

'That maybe I will marry and take over the business eventually.'

'But surely you must have made up your mind about becoming a doctor a long time ago?'

'Well, yes, yes, I had,' she agreed, wishing that she could change the subject.

'So?' Clearly he wasn't going to let it go.

Kirstin took a deep breath. 'I guess his hopes are centred more on the man I might marry than on what my eventual involvement in the actual running of the business might be.'

'Ah,' said Harry knowingly. 'So, who is he—this man your parents think you might marry?'

'His name is Scott Grantham and he's the son of their best friends. We grew up together. He was—is—absolutely mad about boats. He's a professional yachtsman. Takes part in competitive racing; sails all over the world. He's somewhere off New Zealand at the present time.' She hoped that she sounded casual, matter-of-fact, but had the uneasy feeling that her voice was pitched a little higher than usual and sounded quite unnatural.

'And what about you? Do you think he is the man you might marry?'

Kirstin shrugged. 'Who knows? It's what everyone would like.'

'But is it what you would like?'

'I don't know. I'm hoping it may become apparent to us both during this year we are apart.'

'But do you love him?' Harry's eyes narrowed as he looked at her, and Kirstin felt her stomach suddenly churn.

'I don't know that either,' she said flippantly.

'You would, you know,' said Harry softly, 'if you loved him, I mean. Believe me, you would know.'

'Is that the voice of experience speaking?' she asked, still trying to keep her voice light but at the same time only too aware that an image of Harry with Juliet had crept into her mind. It was an image that curiously excited her and she wondered if he was about to enlighten her further about that particular phase in his life. Instead, he merely shrugged.

'It's simply what I've been told,' he said and then, glancing around him and pushing himself away from the worktop, he added, 'Well, if there's nothing else I can do here, I'll leave you to it. If there is anything you want just give me a shout. I shall be in all day, catching up on paper work.'

'Right, Harry. But I'm sure I'll be fine now. And thank you for your help.'

'I'll see you in the morning, then.' He seemed to hesitate for a moment, almost as if he wanted to say more. . .or. . . Kirstin wondered if, perhaps, he expected her to return his hospitality of the previous week.

Surely he couldn't expect that. Not now when she had only just moved in. Maybe later, another time, when she had sorted herself out.

But still he seemed to linger and in the end she said, 'Talking of tomorrow, any chance of you letting me do a surgery on my own yet?'

He shook his head. 'No,' he replied coolly, 'not yet.'

'But Charles let me, after doing only a few with him,' she protested. 'I've done a whole week with you.'

'Before I let you go solo I shall want to sit in with you,' he replied calmly.

She stared at him in dismay. She couldn't think of anything worse than to have him watching her during consultations. 'Is that really necessary?' she asked.

'Maybe not,' he replied, 'but it's the way I operate.'

He went then but left Kirstin dreading the thought of the following day.

CHAPTER EIGHT

KIRSTIN slept badly that night. She tried to put it down to the fact that it was the first night in her new home and that she was in a strange bed, but each time she woke up it was to find Harry Brolin on her mind and it was he who had featured in the lurid dreams which had woken her.

And when, eventually, she abandoned all attempts to sleep and lay awake, staring at the reflection of the quay lights on the ceiling, it was the thought that he was lying only a stone's throw away from her—in his own bed in the same building—that prevented her return to sleep.

She hadn't really meant to tell him about Scott and their long-running relationship; hadn't really wanted him to know. She wasn't sure why—she just felt that it would be more ammunition for him to use to make her feel even more vulnerable.

She and Scott were very fond of each other, and always had been, but Kirstin had secretly doubted that more would ever come of their relationship. When she had told Harry that she didn't know whether she loved Scott or not she had been perfectly honest.

But what was it he had said in reply?

She frowned into the darkness.

That if she was in love, she would know. That was what he had said.

And he, she supposed, would be a pretty good judge of that if Estelle's version of his feelings for Juliet could be believed.

At the thought of Juliet Kirstin found herself wondering just what Harry's feelings were now towards the tall, cool blonde. But now, of course, Juliet was married with a young son, and when at last Kirstin abandoned any further thoughts of sleep and struggled wearily from her bed she realised that for some reason that fact left her with a strange feeling of relief.

Which was utterly ridiculous, she told herself firmly as she showered. After all, what possible difference could it make to her whether Juliet was married or not?

Harry was already in his consulting-room when a little later that morning Kirstin arrived at the Maybury practice.

Eva met her in Reception, bearing a huge pile of patient records in her hands. 'Dr Brolin says you're taking surgery this morning,' she said, eyeing Kirstin up and down as if trying to determine whether or not she was up to this dubious honour. 'He said for us to warn the patients—in case they object,' she added darkly.

'Maybe you should also mention that it is a supervised surgery,' said Kirstin. 'I would imagine Dr Brolin will be very much in control.'

'Well, you can't take chances,' Eva retorted, thrusting the records into Kirstin's arms. Then, in her own indomitable way, she moved forward to the glass partition to sort out the crowd of patients.

As Kirstin made her way to the consulting-room she wondered just who it was who would be taking the chances. Harry, risking his patients to her tender mercies, or she, being thrown to the mob? In the end she gave up trying to figure out Eva's reasoning and pushed open the door.

Harry was on the phone. He glanced up as she came into the room and waved her to the chair he usually sat in, the one directly behind the desk. This morning he was sitting in the chair she had previously used. Nervously she sat down and began looking through the records. It seemed, on first glance, a very mixed surgery.

After a few moments Harry finished his conversation and replaced the receiver.

'All set?' he asked, the disconcerting tawny gaze meeting hers.

'Yes.' Kirstin swallowed. 'Yes, I think so.' She had never felt this nervous with Charles—not even when she'd gone solo.

'Couple of reports here you might be interested in before we start.' Harry picked up some papers on the desk and glanced through them, before handing them to her. 'Casualty letter and follow-up report on Albert Jones.'

'Albert Jones?' Kirstin frowned; the name didn't ring any bells with her.

'The domestic incident we were called to?'

'Oh, yes, Bert,' she said slowly. 'Is he all right?'

'Seems like it. See for yourself.' Harry watched as she scanned the reports, which stated that Bert's wounds had been sutured, that X-rays had not revealed any further injuries and that the patient had also received five units of blood.

'And here's Linda's Casualty report.' Harry handed her another sheet of paper. 'She had a fractured nose, severe bruising to her jaw and had lost a front tooth.'

'What about Tommy?' asked Kirstin, reading the report without looking up. 'Do we know anything about him?'

'Yes, that was Social Services I was speaking to when you came in.' Harry nodded towards the phone. 'Tommy is back in hospital, receiving psychiatric treatment.'

'Well, that's a relief,' said Kirstin. 'He won't be charged with anything, will he?'

'I should say it's highly unlikely. The other guy is facing serious charges, apparently.'

'Serves him right,' said Kirstin.

'You did well that night, you know,' said Harry quietly. 'I meant to tell you again but somehow it got forgotten, what with what happened to Charles, but the way you talked Tommy round was first class.'

Whether or not it was those few words of praise Kirstin didn't know, but quite suddenly her nervousness disappeared and she faced the first patient with positive calm.

The range of patients and ailments was extensive, moving right across the spectrum, from male to female and from the very young—a six-week-old baby with colic—to the very old—an elderly man with prostate problems.

At first she was acutely aware of Harry, sitting slightly behind her, conscious that he might at any moment interrupt her; question her judgement or her decisions in some way.

But he didn't, remaining silent. Her confidence grew, and his presence in the room faded, only returning and falling sharply into focus when one patient—a middle-aged woman—demanded to know if Kirstin was properly qualified and then it was Harry who replied.

'I can assure you, Mrs Boxall,' he said smoothly, 'that Dr Patterson is fully qualified; she is simply doing what we all had to do, myself included, and that is gain experience. If that didn't happen general practitioners would become a dying breed, and where would that leave patients?'

The woman questioned no more, Harry retreated quietly to his corner again and Kirstin carried on, aware now of a warmth somewhere deep inside her that hadn't been there before.

The locum to replace Charles Hardiman arrived that morning, easing the workload considerably on the other partners.

'What's he like?' asked Isabella when Kirstin popped

into the treatment room to replenish the supplies in her medical bag.

'Seems very nice,' replied Kirstin.

'How old?'

'Fiftyish, maybe a bit older.'

'Just our luck.' Isabella sighed. 'Why do we never get one of these handsome young doctors like you see on the telly?'

Kirstin laughed. 'Probably because they aren't doctors—just handsome young actors.'

'How's your surgery been going?' asked Isabella.

'Pretty well, thanks,' replied Kirstin, aware that Val Metcalf had stopped what she was doing and was listening.

'Have you gone solo yet?' Val asked suddenly.

'No.' Kirstin shook her head. 'At least, not for Harry. Charles let me but Harry is rather harder to please.'

'He probably likes sitting in with you all day,' said Isabella wickedly, and when Val scowled she went on, 'And what's all this we've been hearing about Harry finding you an apartment?'

'Yes. . .' Kirstin hesitated, wondering how much they knew. 'Yes, he did. And I'm very grateful. Being new to the area I didn't really know where to start.'

'So, where is it, exactly?' Val's eyes narrowed slightly. 'This new apartment of yours?'

'Er. . .down by the docks,' replied Kirstin.

'Isn't that where Harry himself lives?' asked Isabella quickly.

If Kirstin had thought she was going to escape without further explanation she was sadly mistaken. 'Yes, it is,' she admitted then, before the inevitable question was asked, she went on, 'Actually, my apartment—well, it's a flat really, a studio flat—is in the same complex. . .'

'As Harry Brolin's, you mean?' Val was quick to seize on the fact.

Kirstin nodded, suddenly feeling sorry for Val who so obviously had carried a torch for Harry for so long without the sentiment being reciprocated in any way. 'Yes, in fact Harry told me about it when I first came here, but at that time there was no real hurry to move from the Hardimans' so I did nothing about it. I was lucky it was still there when I had to change my plans quickly,' she added.

'So, is it nice?' asked Isabella. 'Those warehouses certainly look nice from the outside, and I suppose they have a river view as well.'

'Not all of them,' said Kirstin. 'Mine doesn't because it's at the back of the building but Harry's has magnificent views. . .you must both come over some time and see mine—' She broke off as Val suddenly turned and stomped out of the treatment room.

'Oh, dear,' said Kirstin, 'what have I said now? I do seem to keep putting my foot in it where Val is concerned.'

Isabella chuckled wickedly. 'Her imagination's probably working overtime, wondering just what you were doing in Harry Brolin's flat.'

'I can assure you it was nothing.' Kirstin felt herself reddening, but Isabella merely laughed.

'Don't worry. I believe you. If the rumours are anything to go by you would be quite safe with him, anyway.'

'Whatever do you mean?' Kirstin stared at her.

'Oh, nothing bizarre.' Isabella grinned. 'Simply that our Dr Brolin is what is known as a one-woman man. Apparently he was engaged once. She let him down badly and he's not bothered with anyone else since.'

'Do you know who he was engaged to?' asked Kirstin, wondering if the story was common knowledge amongst the staff.

'Well, again, rumour has it that it was Charles

Hardiman's daughter,' said Isabella, then added, 'but it was years ago—at least ten years. None of the rest of the staff have been here that long, except for Bruce, and he isn't talking so we don't really know for sure.'

She went back to Harry's consulting-room to go through the day's house calls with him, but she found herself wondering if what Isabella had said was, indeed, true. It certainly seemed to fit in with what Estelle had said about how he had worshipped Juliet, but it also seemed a little hard to believe that it had put him off other women. Ten years, or possibly more, was a very long time.

As Kirstin became involved in the life of the practice the days seemed to slip by with alarming rapidity. Eventually Harry allowed her to go solo with surgeries.

'You're on your own,' he told her one morning.

'Oh, right.' She didn't know whether she was pleased or alarmed while he, apparently sensing something of her apprehension, said, 'Don't worry—I shall only be next door. Shout if there's anything you want. If you're not sure of something—ask. OK?'

'OK.' As her gaze met his she smiled and the expression in the tawny eyes softened. His attitude towards her seemed to have changed since they'd been working together. He did not seem as abrasive as he had when she had first arrived, and as the days passed and slipped into weeks she even began to feel that she was earning his grudging respect.

Her feelings for him, however, remained unchanged. As a man she didn't particularly like him; his presence still disturbed her, whether in the surgery, alongside him on house calls or when they met, however briefly, at the apartment.

As a doctor, however, she was slowly being forced to

admit that he was good. He knew his patients and was
tuned in to their needs.

As for the rest of the staff they had also come to accept
her, even though with some it seemed to be rather a
gradual process as Kirstin herself learnt the many facets
of each individual's behaviour and the idiosyncrasies
which could only be recognised through day-to-day
contact.

Bruce, for example, was vague but a born worrier,
while Rhannie had a calm acceptance of life.

As time passed Kirstin even gradually came to accept
Eva, realising that she was, indeed, an asset to this particular practice. Her friendship with Isabella grew
stronger as they discovered they had several things in
common and eventually even Val began to thaw a little
towards her.

Charles Hardiman was finally discharged from
hospital into community care, although he was severely
paralysed, and Harry was called to visit him.

Kirstin was accompanying him on all house calls and
it had previously been agreed between them that she
should do the consultation, only referring to Harry if she
should find herself out of her depth.

When they arrived at Fir Tree Lodge Kirstin felt her
apprehension mounting. She had been on edge ever since
Harry had told her of the visit. She wasn't really sure
why until they were standing on the doorstep, Harry had
rung the bell and Juliet opened the door.

Then she knew that her apprehension had nothing to
do with visiting Charles or Estelle: nothing to do with
any medical problems which might arise or test her
knowledge in front of Harry. It was purely and simply
because of this woman's presence in the house. This
woman who stood before them now, dressed in a navy
cotton jumper over a white shirt and faded blue jeans
and with her blonde hair in a loose bob. This woman, of

whom she had learnt so much in the short time she had been at Maybury.

'Harry.' The blue eyes softened, and the mouth curved into a smile. 'We were expecting you. Come in.'

'Thank you, Juliet.' He walked into the hall then turned, remembering. 'You've met Kirstin, haven't you?' he said.

'Yes,' Juliet smiled. 'It was Kirstin's quick thinking that saved my father's life.'

'Yes, indeed.' A smile also crossed Harry's features, and for one awful moment as she followed them through the house Kirstin thought that he must have told Juliet about that night and of how angry he had been with her. She dismissed the thought almost as soon as it was formed. She was becoming paranoid, she told herself severely.

The sunny breakfast room at the back of the house which overlooked the garden had been adapted into a bedroom for Charles. Estelle was standing by a small table, folding a pile of freshly laundered towels. She turned to greet them.

'Harry, Kirstin. It's good to see you both.' She looked tired, Kirstin thought, tired and drawn. but Estelle's appearance—understandable as it was—did nothing to prepare Kirstin for the parody of Charles, sitting in a high-backed chair in front of the window.

He appeared to be watching two blackbirds on a bird table on the patio and did nothing to acknowledge their arrival or, indeed, even to indicate that he knew they were there. He looked at least ten years older—his hair, once silver-grey, was now white and wispy, his body was shrunk into the very depths of the chair, his right arm was withered and useless and his face was twisted, the expression distorted.

Kirstin tried desperately, but unsuccessfully, to fight back the tears that sprang to her eyes, and at the same time struggled to control the lump that rose in her throat. She hadn't known Charles Hardiman for very long but the time she had shared with him had been quality time of the highest calibre.

He had been the one to welcome her to Maybury, had been kindness itself, offering his home to her along with all the knowledge and expertise of a lifetime of caring.

For the moment it was as if she, too, was rendered not only speechless but useless. Harry threw her a quick glance and must have summed up the situation for he moved forward, rested his case on the table and opened it.

'Hello there, old friend,' he said softly to Charles. 'How's it going?'

In the end all Kirstin could do was to leave the medical side of the visit to Harry while she simply observed.

Carefully, tenderly almost, Harry examined the man who had been both mentor and friend then, leaving Juliet to dress him again, he questioned Estelle about Charles's diet, bodily functions, range of movements and physiotherapy.

While Harry wrote prescriptions for pain control, laxatives and decongestants Juliet went out of the room, and Estelle turned to Kirstin.

'Have you settled into your apartment?' she asked.

'Yes, yes, thank you.' Kirstin swallowed and nodded, desperately trying to pull herself together.

'And how are you getting on with Harry?' Estelle's expression softened as he gaze fell on Harry, who was still scribbling furiously. 'Not treating you too harshly, I hope?'

He glanced up, looking at Kirstin from under his brows.

'Oh, no,' she said quickly, 'no, of course not.'

Harry finished writing, closed his case and, standing up, briefly touched Charles on the shoulder. Then, without another word, he went quickly from the room.

Kirstin allowed her gaze to meet Estelle's and saw the understanding there in the older woman's eyes. Neither voiced what they were feeling but Kirstin moved round in front of Charles and, summoning from somewhere a firm voice, said, 'I'll be in again to see you, Charles, and I have forgiven you, just about, for leaving me to Harry Brolin's tender mercies.' She crouched down as she spoke, looking directly into the tired blue eyes.

And, just for one moment, she swore she saw a spark of recognition there—a response to her humour. Taking his left hand, she squeezed it and there was a slight but unmistakable tightening in reply, then, releasing his hand, she straightened up and moved rapidly away from the chair.

Harry was in the hall with Juliet—the two heads, dark and fair, close together. They drew apart as Estelle and Kirstin joined them but it was obvious that they had shared a moment of deep emotion.

'I'll be in again, Estelle,' said Harry as they walked to the front door, 'and, don't forget, if there's anything you need—anything at all—just shout.' He paused, one hand on the door handle. 'Is Matthew all right?' he asked suddenly, turning to Juliet.

She nodded. 'Yes, he's fine. He's with Paul. We thought it best as it's during term-time. Paul brings him over at weekends.'

Kirstin walked out to the car, leaving them talking.

Harry joined her a few minutes later and, as the two women went back into the house and shut the door, he drove sharply away without looking back. Sitting silently beside him, Kirstin wondered what his thoughts were; what they could possibly be in this situation.

At last she dared a glance at his profile as he drove through the busy lunchtime traffic. It was set and uncompromising, giving nothing away. Eventually she dared to speak; to break the silence.

'I'm sorry I was so useless back there,' she said.

'It's OK.' His voice was quiet, the tone resigned somehow.

She was surprised; she had not expected that. She wasn't really sure what she had expected, possibly anger—derision even for her lack of professionalism—but certainly not this.

'No,' she said, 'it isn't OK. Not really. I just couldn't cope. It was seeing Charles like that. I knew. . .should have known what to expect, but it was different. . .far worse than I had expected.'

While she was speaking they had reached the centre and Charles unlocked the compound, drove inside and switched off the engine. Neither of them moved or made any attempt to get out of the car.

'These things happen,' he said slowly.

'But I should have been prepared. I should have been able to overcome my own feelings. . .'

'Maybe. But it's not always that easy, especially when one is personally involved with a patient.'

'I should still have been able to cope,' she insisted. 'And when it comes to personal involvement. . .well, you were far more involved than me. It must be really distressing for you to see Charles like that.'

'Yes.' He gripped the steering-wheel so tightly that his knuckles showed white. 'Yes, it is.'

'So, I should have been the one to cope. . .the one to get on with it. I shouldn't have left it all to you.'

'It's at times like this that experience counts.'

'Even so.' She was angry with herself and, turning her head away, she bit her lip.

'Kirstin.' His voice was low. 'Don't be so hard on yourself,' he said unexpectedly.

She found herself wishing he would be angry. Somehow she would have coped better with that; would have found it more predictable. This uncharacteristic compassion was almost her undoing. Then, as if that wasn't enough, she felt his hand on hers.

Dumbfounded, she remained perfectly still. This couldn't be happening. She must be dreaming. At any moment she would wake up and Harry would be nagging her for something she had done wrong.

But it wasn't a dream; it was happening. His hand, warm and comforting, was covering her own where it lay in her lap and briefly, unbelievably, his thumb gently began stroking her knuckles.

Then it was over. Abruptly he withdrew his hand and said, 'Come on. We have work to do. Life goes on. And we have a practice to run.'

When Kirstin looked back, the day when they visited Charles and that moment afterwards in the practice car park were to be turning points but at the time, of course, she had no idea of that.

It was only as time marched on, as spring blossomed and slipped gently into early summer, that she realised that a change was slowly taking place.

Harry still nagged her; at times got exasperated with her; sometimes praised her, sometimes reproached her or mocked her for her naïvety, but underneath there was a difference. A difference that became more and more apparent in the most unexpected ways—like Sunday mornings, for example.

It was Kirstin's habit when they weren't on call on a Sunday to have a short lie-in, then to shower, dress in track suit and trainers and jog along the quay to the mini-market where she picked up the Sunday papers and some fresh orange juice, before jogging back to her apartment.

On one particular Sunday—a glorious morning when the mist was just rising and sunlight sparkled on the river; when a profusion of flowers tumbled from the hanging baskets around the pub opposite The Warehouse and the sound of church bells filled the air—Kirstin had just returned from the shop with her purchases when a shout hailed her from above.

Glancing up, she saw Harry standing on his balcony.

'Hello.' Shading her eyes from the sun with her papers, she stared up at him.

'Care for some breakfast?' he called casually.

'I've just been to buy some orange juice.'

'Good. I'm nearly out of it. Come on up.'

She'd gone up; without hesitation, she'd gone up and joined him on his balcony.

'It's silly not to share this view when it's there,' he said, carrying toast, marmalade and fresh coffee from his kitchen and placing them on the balcony table.

And it had become something of a ritual, their off-duty Sunday mornings. Kirstin continued to collect the papers and the orange juice, but it became accepted that she would join him and together they would sit in the sunshine, eating breakfast, reading the papers, drinking endless cups of coffee and enjoying the view.

It had become so established that one Sunday morning when she awoke and heard rain against the window-pane she was bitterly disappointed. Her disappointment was short-lived, however, for no sooner had she got dressed than her phone rang.

'It's raining,' he said, 'so a balcony breakfast might not be a good idea. But the view's still there so there's no reason why we shouldn't sit at the window.'

And they had—at the dining-table. The view was still there, although the river was grey and the far bank shrouded in mist. And even if it wasn't quite the same as their breakfasts in the sun it was still good.

Kirstin hardly dared analyse just why it was so good but deep down she was beginning to realise that just being with Harry had something to do with it, just as she was also beginning to realise how simply being with him was starting to affect every other part of her life as well.

CHAPTER NINE

THE day started the same as any other, with no hint of all that was to follow.

It was one of those warm June days when there was barely a cloud in the sky, the sort of day that made Kirstin think of white sails on the Solent and sunlight sparkling on the water. She almost had to force herself into the right frame of mind for surgery, and when she finally arrived at the centre it was to find two police cars parked outside.

'Break-in,' said Eva flatly, by way of explanation.

'Did they take much?' asked Kirstin, looking round at the shattered window and splintered wood behind Reception.

'No,' Eva shook her head. 'Not much here for them to take at night. They were after drugs, of course—and prescription pads. Looks like they took an axe to that door—the blighters. Wish I could get my hands on them; I know what I'd do to them.'

Kirstin nodded. She had no doubt either what Eva would do to the culprits, but she had little time to contemplate it further for Reception was rapidly filling up.

Every surgery and clinic for that day was fully booked, each with a list of emergency extras. It was becoming a general rule that Kirstin saw the extras each day, together with any temporary residents. By the very nature of these lists it was inevitable that most cases she dealt with were acute situations, meaning that she saw little of ongoing or chronic ailments. Harry was aware of this and occasionally, by way of change, would switch surgeries with her. That morning was one such time and Kirstin found herself with a list made up entirely of Harry's patients.

He was, as she had already found out on numerous occasions, a hard act to follow and the first few minutes of each consultation invariably were taken up with placating the patient, who had been expecting to see Dr Brolin.

There were, of course, the inevitable few who, seizing the opportunity of a fresh face, sought a second opinion on a long-standing problem, but most remained loyal.

By the end of the morning Kirstin felt quite drained and although that particular surgery might be over she was faced with referrals and a mountain of paperwork to be completed.

She was only halfway through when Harry called her to accompany him on house visits. Even that list seemed heavier than usual that day and included a call to Maggie Burns on the top floor of her tower block.

Maggie had been experiencing recurrent water infections and that morning was in bed, complaining of severe pain in her side and in the small of her back. Her daughter, Tracy, let Harry and Kirstin into the flat.

Kirstin examined Maggie, noting that she was feverish and shivery with a temperature of 39 degrees.

Harry stood back, talking quietly to Tracy, while Kirstin completed her examination. When she had finished she stood up and moved away from the bed, while Harry raised his eyebrows questioningly, at her.

'I would say pyelonephritis,' said Kirstin.

Harry nodded. 'Treatment?'

'Normally I would say sulphonamides or antibiotics and bedrest, followed by an IVP, but. . .' She hesitated, glancing back at Maggie.

'Yes?' prompted Harry.

'In Maggie's case, taking into account all her other problems, I think a spell in a medical ward wouldn't come amiss. Her arthritic pain is worse, her breathing is bad and she's hardly eating at all.'

Harry nodded again. 'I agree. Perhaps you'd like to make the necessary arrangements. The phone is in the sitting-room.'

Ambulance Control knew her now and there was no hesitation when Kirstin requested a vehicle, any more than there was from the houseman she spoke to at Maybury City General who told her that a bed would be waiting for Maggie on the medical ward.

'I doubt it will be for too long,' she explained to Tracy, 'but I do think your mum needs a few things sorting out, and they will do an IVP—a kidney X-ray—at the same time.'

'Thanks,' said Tracy. 'This flat don't help.'

'If I can do something about that I will,' said Kirstin fiercely, 'but I think for the time being a hospital bed will have to suffice.'

'Quite the crusader,' said Harry a little later when they were in the car and on their way back to the centre and afternoon surgery.

'I still get angry about these situations,' muttered Kirstin. 'I can't help it; I just do.'

'Thank God they had a bed for Maggie. I wouldn't have liked to have been that SHO on the other end of the line if they hadn't.'

She threw him a sharp glance and when he turned his head briefly and glanced at her there was amusement in his eyes.

'Maybe you've given up trying to do anything in these impossible situations,' she snapped, 'but I haven't.'

'Good for you.' He sounded serious, but as they got out of the car she had the distinct impression that he was mocking her again.

The day ground relentlessly on, with Harry taking his own afternoon surgery and Kirstin taking an impossibly long list of extras which were supposed to be emergencies but which made her wonder from time to time—especially the case of the man who told her he had a ringing noise in his ears and when she enquired as to how long it had been there his reply was, 'Since the Second World War'.

When at last she finished she made her way wearily into Reception. 'Tell me that's the end,' she said to Hayley. The girl turned from the computer screen on the desk to face her, and Kirstin was surprised to see that her usual cheeky expression was missing.

'Is there something wrong?' Kirstin asked, gradually becoming aware that it wasn't only Hayley who was acting in this way but that the rest of the staff also appeared subdued.

'Dr Brolin's been called out,' said Hayley shortly. 'An emergency visit.'

'Oh? He didn't say,' said Kirstin.

'He didn't stop for anything,' said Eva bluntly, overhearing as she crossed Reception to close a window.

Intuition warning her that something momentous had happened, Kirstin turned back to Hayley.

'It was Dr Hardiman,' the girl said.

'Charles. . .?' Kirstin's heart dropped like a stone.

'Yes.' Hayley nodded. 'Another stroke, by the sound of it. Mrs Hardiman rang—she sounded awful.'

Without another word Kirstin turned and went slowly back to her room where, for the next hour, she tried desperately and without success to concentrate on the paperwork she had previously abandoned.

She heard Harry return. Heard his car as it drove past her window on its way through the alley to the compound. She put down her pen and waited.

Five minutes later her door opened.

Fearfully she looked up at him as he stood there in the doorway. His tie was undone, his jacket was crumpled and he looked desperately tired but there was another

expression in his eyes—one she'd never seen before—
and she knew what he was going to say before he even
opened his mouth.

'I was too late,' he said. 'He was dead before I
got there.'

'Oh, Harry.' She half rose out of her chair. Instinc-
tively, her intention was to go to him, to comfort him,
but something in his face stopped her and she sank back
down into the chair again.

'I'm so sorry,' she said quietly at last.

'Another massive CVA,' he said, coming right into
the room and tossing a set of notes—presumably
Charles's—onto the desk in a hopeless gesture. 'Absolutely nothing to be done.' He walked to the window and
stood, gazing out at the red brick wall beyond.

'How is Estelle?' she asked after a moment.

'Shocked. Devastated,' he replied, without turning
round. 'I didn't even feel capable of comforting her.'

'And Juliet?'

'I think Juliet anticipated it. She's a nurse and she's
nursed many stroke victims in the past. It just seems so
unfair.' He turned and looked at Kirstin. 'He didn't even
reach retirement. A man like that who's given so much
to the community.'

He paused, took a deep breath and went on, 'They had
so many plans, he and Estelle. A trip to Canada to see
his brother. A cruise on the Nile. . .I don't know. . .I'm
sorry.' He gave a gesture of helplessness. 'I just can't
seem to take it in.'

'It was a shock for you as well,' said Kirstin. She did
stand up then. 'Let me get you something. . .a hot drink
perhaps. . .?'

'I should be used to this sort of thing,' he said, taking
no notice of her question.

'Just because you're a doctor it doesn't make you
immune to shock or to grief,' she said quietly. 'And,

from what I've seen, I would say that Charles was a very special person to you.'

He was silent for a moment then, passing one hand over his face, he sighed and nodded. 'Yes,' he said, 'he was. He took me under his wing when I was at medical school, still a student. He was a bit like a father to me, really. Then he vouched for me after I'd qualified and wanted to become a partner. The others thought I was too young, too raw, but Charles spoke up for me. . .persuaded them to give me a chance. . .'

'And at one time wasn't he almost your father-in-law as well?' said Kirstin softly. She was watching him closely when she said it and she saw the tawny eyes darken before he glanced up sharply.

'Who told you that?' he said.

'Estelle,' she replied shortly.

'Oh.' He nodded, and after a moment he added, 'Yes, Juliet and I were engaged once. . .a long time ago. . .' He sighed again and for one moment it seemed to Kirstin as if he were right back there in the past in that time when he was a new young partner in the practice; when he and Juliet were to be married.

Then abruptly, with an almost visible effort, he attempted to pull himself together.

'We still have an evening family planning clinic to do,' he said wearily. 'Have you had anything to eat?'

Kirstin shook her head. 'Not yet, but Hayley's gone out for a take-away for us.'

It was very late when they finally got away that evening.

Harry followed her in his car to The Warehouse. Kirstin was conscious of him close behind her all the way, finding the fact strangely comforting. She had already decided that she would ask him in for a nightcap when they got home. Whether he would accept or refuse, she didn't know, but when at last they parked their cars, entered the building and stepped into the lift Harry's mobile phone suddenly rang and it seemed that the day was far from over.

She watched him as he took the call—the fatigue on his features, the deep lines etched from nose to mouth—and her heart went out to him.

'That was the police,' he said, replacing the aerial. 'They've recovered a body and want me to certify the death.'

Kirstin didn't hesitate for one moment. 'I'll come with you,' she said.

'There's no need,' he replied. 'You can't do anything.'

'Maybe not. But I'm coming all the same.'

'You've had one hell of a day.'

'So have you.'

He didn't argue any more, just accepted the fact that she was going with him. They didn't even get out of the lift, just pressed the button for the ground floor again.

'We'll take my car,' he said.

Her tiredness seemed to vanish and a sudden surge of adrenalin took over as she sat beside him.

They sped through the night to another Docklands site, but one much further down river than The Warehouse. This site was much closer to the estuary and they were guided to the location by the inevitable flashing blue lights of the police and rescue services.

A body had been recovered from the river and had been drawn up onto a narrow band of shingle. The police had erected a couple of arc lights and had already cordoned off the area. The sergeant in charge greeted Harry by name, nodded to Kirstin and led the way behind the makeshift canvas screen that shielded the body.

'It was spotted by a chap, fishing,' said the policeman, lifting back the sheet of black polythene. 'Not a pretty sight, miss.' He glanced at Kirstin. 'Been in the water for some time, I'd say.'

Kirstin took a deep breath and forced herself to look down. She'd seen many dead bodies during her training but not one that had been recovered from the river.

It was grotesquely swollen, the skin a purplish-blue in colour, but it was unmistakably the body of a young woman. Her hair, although matted and covered with slime and weed, had once been blonde and at first glance it looked to Kirstin as if she'd been in her mid to late twenties—about the same age as herself.

She watched silently as Harry made his examination, moving closer when he glanced up at her.

'She's been dead for some time,' he said. 'At least three or four days, possibly more by the condition of the body, but. . .' he glanced at his watch '. . .I certify death at 22:00 hours.'

'Did she drown?' Kirstin's voice came out as little more than a whisper.

'No.' Harry shook his head. 'She was hit on the back of the head—see here.' He turned the body and revealed an ugly gash at the base of the skull. 'And there are marks here, around her neck, that could be consistent with strangulation. The post mortem will show more.'

'So it's a job for the CID boys?' said the sergeant and when Harry nodded he went on, 'Can't say I'm surprised. I'll get on to them and they'll send their pathologist over.'

'Do you have any idea who she was?' asked Harry as, with a last glance at the girl's body, they followed the policeman away from the shingle beach and back onto the quayside.

'We think she may be a young woman by the name of Sandie Markham,' he replied, then added,' A local prostitute. She was reported missing two days ago. We won't know for sure until identification has taken place. Anyway, Doc, we won't keep you any longer now. Thanks for your time. Goodbye, miss.'

'Goodbye,' said Kirstin weakly. Suddenly, to her horror, she was beginning to feel quite faint and by the time she got into Harry's car she was shaking.

What in the world was wrong with her? She was supposed to be a doctor, for heaven's sake.

She wasn't going to be much use to anyone if she was going to keel over every time she saw something remotely distressing. She gazed out of the window, struggling for control, as the Docklands lights passed her unseeing eyes in a blur.

'Do you get much of that sort of thing to deal with?' she asked at last when Harry had remained silent for much of the drive back to The Warehouse.

'More than there used to be, I hate to say,' he replied grimly.

'She was only about my age,' said Kirstin shakily. 'It's such a waste. . .what do you think happened to her?'

'Who knows?' Harry replied abruptly, but his tone was gentle. 'It's not for me to reason why. All that's required of me is to establish that life is extinct—'

'But you must wonder!' she interrupted sharply. 'You must. . .!'

He threw her a glance; must have seen her distress, which she was finding difficult to hide.

'Yes,' he said quietly at last, 'of course I wonder. I wouldn't be human if I didn't but, like I said, officially it isn't for me to say—'

'So what about unofficially?' Again she interrupted him. 'What do you think happened to her—unofficially?'

He shrugged. 'You really want to know?'

'Yes. Yes, Harry, I do.' She was aware that her voice had taken on a higher pitch—sounded agitated—but there was nothing she could do about it.

'Well,' he said and there was a resigned note in his voice now, 'there's little doubt that she was murdered. Whether she was hit over the head first or strangled, we won't know until after the post mortem. . .but at a guess, and it is only a guess, I would say she was strangled first. The blow on the head probably came later—before she was dumped in the river—just to make sure.'

'But who could do that? Who could do such a thing?' To Kirstin's horror, she was shaking again. She had no idea why. She had read about this sort of thing countless times in the papers. Seen it all on the television or in films. But this was different. This was real. This was happening. And she was involved. She and Harry.

'There are all manner of people who could do it,' said Harry. 'An ex-boyfriend. Her husband, perhaps.'

'But the policeman said he thought she might be a prostitute. . .'

'All right, then, a jealous boyfriend or husband, a punter or maybe someone who has a grudge against prostitutes. I don't know. You read the papers, Kirstin; these things happen all the time.'

'I know.' Her breath caught in her throat. 'I'm sorry. I'm just being silly. It's just that she was so young and there was something about her, her hair I think, that reminded me of a friend of mine—a girl I went to school with. . .I'm sorry,' she said again.

'It's OK,' said Harry softly. 'And it was your first time for that sort of thing.'

'I don't somehow think I would make a very good police doctor,' she said shakily as he drew into The Warehouse car park and switched off the engine.

'Nonsense,' he replied. 'The first time I went to the scene of a murder I disgraced myself completely and threw up everywhere.'

'Did you?' She stared at him in the dark in astonishment.

'Yes, but I was all right after a brandy,' he said quietly, 'which is what I'm going to give you right now.'

'Oh, but. . .' She was about to say that she didn't

usually drink spirits, but he wasn't listening. Instead, as they got out of the car and walked towards the apartments, he took her arm and with one hand firmly beneath her elbow he guided her inside.

For the second time that night they took the lift to the third floor. This time, however, Harry's phone remained silent and together they went into his apartment.

Closing the door behind them, he made as if to take her jacket and stood very close behind her as he began to ease it from her shoulders, but then he stopped and, instead, he said, 'You're cold; you're shivering, Kirstin. Keep this on for the time being.' Firmly he pulled her jacket up again, his hands lingering just for a second at the back of her neck.

Involuntarily she stiffened at his touch; at the feel of his hands against her bare skin.

'Come over here.' Taking her hand and chafing it between his own, he led her to the sofa. 'Sit down, and I'll get you that brandy.'

Taking off his own jacket, he crossed to the kitchen area of his apartment while Kirstin sat in one corner of the sofa—desperately trying to control her shivering and the chattering of her teeth.

Whatever must he think of her? She was behaving like an utter wimp, all her previous protestations of being a fully qualified, competent doctor scattered now to the four winds.

He was back almost immediately with two brandy glasses, a generous measure in each.

'No arguing,' he said as he handed her a glass. 'Doctor's orders—for medicinal purposes.'

She managed a weak smile but, on taking the glass, her hand was shaking so much that she couldn't prevent her fingers touching his.

'Th-th-thank you,' she stammered. 'I'm s-sorry about this. I'm n-not usually s-such a w-w-wimp.'

He stood and watched her, cradling his glass in one hand and rocking slightly on his heels.

'I told you,' he said at last, after she'd taken a sip of the brandy, 'you're not to worry about it. It's been a hellish day one way and another. . .what with this last wretched business and. . .with. . . Charles.'

To her horror, at the mention of Charles Kirstin felt her eyes fill with tears. 'I know,' she gulped, searching by the side of the sofa for the small table she knew was there to set her glass on. 'I know.' Fumbling in her pocket, she drew out a crumpled tissue and wiped her eyes.

'I kn-know,' she said again, managing to continue at last. 'It's been awful, but it's been f-far worse for you. I sh-should be comforting you, and here it is. . .the other way round.'

Setting his own glass down, he sat beside her on the sofa and—putting one arm around her shoulders—he drew her against him. By this time her tears were flowing quite freely and in the end she gave up the battle to stop them.

Stretching behind him, Harry took a clean white handkerchief from his jacket, which was draped over the back of the sofa, and gently he wiped away the tears from her cheeks.

'I'm glad you are grieving for Charles,' he said softly, 'and, yes, he was very special to me, but I like to think he was special to you as well.'

'Oh, he was,' she gulped, 'he was.'

'Here, I do want you to drink this, you know.' Putting the handkerchief in his pocket, he reached over the side of the sofa, retrieved her glass and handed it to her again.

Without a word she obeyed him and surprisingly as she swallowed the liquid the warmth seemed to flow into her very veins.

Gradually she stopped shaking.

Harry watched her then, finishing his own brandy in one swallow, he waited until she had also finished before he took her glass and set it back on the table.

She expected him to stand up and prepared herself to do the same but, instead, she felt his arm around her once more and he drew her back with him into the depths of the sofa.

'I really think I should. . .' she began to protest but he silenced her; gently, but firmly, he silenced her.

'Just rest awhile,' he said.

And, suddenly, she did. Suddenly that was all she wanted to do as the fight went out of her. Now she was quite content to lean against him; feel the warmth and strength of his arm around her, protecting her, comforting her.

She had drunk the brandy far too quickly, she knew that. She was unaccustomed to drinking spirits, as it was, and downing it as she had—almost in one go—it was hardly surprising that it had gone straight to her head.

But, quite apart from all that, the most surprising thing of all was how natural it felt, how right, to be here with Harry like this—on his sofa, in his apartment, with her head on his shoulder, with the feel of him, the warmth of his body penetrating his thin cotton shirt, and with the scent of him which seemed to fill her slightly befuddled senses.

It had been a long time since she'd been this close to a man.

Then it had been Scott, dear Scott. She loved him; she'd always loved him; ever since their nursery days she'd loved him.

But it hadn't felt like this.

This feeling of excitement that was gathering—this was quite different, quite new and slightly unreal.

Surely it must be something to do with the brandy.

But even before Harry tilted her face towards him with

his free hand Kirstin was trying to battle with the sudden surge of desire that had sprung from deep inside her, a surge so strong that by the time his mouth covered hers in a kiss at first tentative her response was so spontaneous, so positive that she didn't know who was the more surprised.

The kiss deepened, with Harry exploring, questing, obviously liking what he found and arousing her even further until, to her disappointment, he abruptly drew away.

His arms stayed around her, however, forcing her to remain where she was as the clamourings of her body very gradually subsided again.

She was too tired, too weary to question her reactions or to even try to understand his motives. Somewhere at the back of her mind she was only too aware that the kiss they had shared had not simply been one of comfort. It might have started as one, but it had ended as something quite different.

She would have to think about it later. But not now. She was too tired, too drowsy.

For the moment she was quite content to simply lie here with Harry, warm and safe.

In a minute she would get up, go to her own apartment, but not just yet.

Another five minutes surely wouldn't matter one way or the other.

CHAPTER TEN

KIRSTIN moved slightly, then pulled the duvet more snugly around her.

The bed was warm, she had been enjoying her dream and the alarm clock hadn't actually gone off yet so there was no immediate urgency to get up.

She tried to get back into her dream.

It had been something to do with a boat. Probably the family boat at Bembridge, or maybe Scott's boat. She had been leaning over the side and laughing, and there had been a party going on behind her.

Harry Brolin had been there.

No, surely she was mistaken. Not Harry. Not at home on the Isle of Wight. Harry belonged here in tough Maybury and the docks, not at home in her world of yachts and marinas.

But, no, he had been there—she was sure of it.

He had been close to her, very close, and she had been enjoying the dream.

But was it the fact that she was on board a boat again or had it been the fact that Harry was with her that had made the dream so enjoyable? She wasn't really sure, but it seemed unlikely that the latter could be the case. After all, she and Harry didn't even like each other.

Ah, but it was in real life that they didn't like each other—dreams were different. Dreams conjured up all sorts of interesting improbabilities. . .and fantasies.

Maybe, she thought, if she concentrated really hard she could get back into the dream.

She had been looking over the side of the boat, staring into the water. It must have been the sea and not the river because the water was clear and she could almost see the bottom.

Harry had been close, really close, almost touching her. No, not almost. He had been touching her.

He had been leaning over her, his body—hard and aroused—pressed against hers and his hands gripping her upper arms.

But why? What had he been doing? Or about to do?

Had he been trying to prevent her from falling overboard, or had there been another reason for his closeness?

She squirmed as a sudden shaft of desire shot through her but the dream had gone; had slipped away to be filed with the thousands of others in her subconscious.

Was she never to know what happened next?

Had she straightened up? Had she turned to face him and slipped naturally into his arms? And, if so, what had happened then?

He had been aroused, so had she—she knew that much. Would he have taken her there and then?

She squirmed again, in frustration this time, and drew her knees up until she was in the foetal position.

The dream had gone now; she was awake and there was no knowing what would have happened. She was aware of a deep sense of disappointment.

It would have been intriguing to find out how Harry Brolin made love.

Strange, she thought as her frustration subsided, that the alarm hadn't gone off. She knew it was daylight; could see it through her eyelids.

Maybe she had forgotten to set the alarm the night before. Maybe she'd overslept.

Opening one eye, she looked at the bedside table.

Her clock wasn't there.

She frowned and lifted her head. Not only was the clock not there, the table with its bedside lamp wasn't there either.

With a stab of alarm she sat up and wildly looked around her.

This wasn't her bedroom.

She looked down. These weren't her sheets. Hers were pink. These were royal blue.

Where the hell was she?

The room was bathed in sunlight and, twisting her head, Kirstin looked behind her. There were high arched windows behind the bed and, beyond, a view of the river.

A soft mist hung over the far bank and a tug, chugging gently through the water, sounded its hooter as if in welcome.

Then it all came rushing back to her and she knew exactly where she was. The events of the previous day flashed through her mind—Charles's death, the police call, the body in the river, her own reactions, Harry's response.

He had kissed her.

That memory hit her with a thud.

He had kissed her, held her in his arms and it had all felt as natural as if it happened all the time. They had been right here in this flat.

But not in the bedroom.

They had been downstairs on the sofa.

How had she got up here, for heaven's sake? And in his bed! She certainly didn't remember that.

Wildly she looked down at herself. She was wearing the thin cotton blouse she had worn to work the previous day and her briefs, and that was all. Where were her skirt and her jacket?

Frantically she looked round and there, on a chair, she saw her pink suit—the jacket around the back of the chair, the skirt neatly folded across the seat and her shoes tidily tucked underneath.

But how had they got there? She didn't remember taking them off; was certain, in fact, that she hadn't. So that meant that it must have been Harry who had done so.

And where was he now, for goodness' sake? Where had he spent the night? Surely, surely he hadn't. . .?

Even as the thought struck her Kirstin's gaze flew to the empty place beside her in the large double bed.

Was it crumpled? Was that an indentation in the pillow or was it simply her imagination? Had he slept there beside her all night? Had he actually done that? Undressed her, then himself, and got into bed with her? Surely even Harry Brolin wouldn't be that arrogant.

Or would he? What of her dream? That strange, unreal dream she'd had. He had featured heavily in that and it had been erotic, to say the least.

But just supposing it hadn't been a dream at all; supposing it had been real—that the feel of his body against her, his obvious arousal, had been a reality.

If it had been real, she had remembered it. What of the rest of it—the part she couldn't remember?

Could they actually have made love? Right here in this bed?

That was impossible. Ridiculous, she told herself sharply. She would have known. How could she not have been aware of that?

But, a little voice persisted inside her head, she hadn't been aware of him bringing her up the stairs to this bed; hadn't been aware of him undressing her, so maybe she'd been unaware of the rest.

But, if that was the case, why hadn't she been aware? It was almost as if she'd been drunk.

The brandy. That was it. She had been drunk.

But she'd only had one, for goodness' sake. Well, maybe two—it had been a very generous measure.

Yes, that had to have been it—the brandy. She had been aware of it going to her head soon after she'd drunk it. . . So it either had to be that. . .or Harry Brolin had slipped something into it!

Surely, even he wouldn't do something like that. Why would he?

To get her into his bed? To make love to her without her knowledge? Had it happened? Could the dream not have been a dream at all. . .?

'Ah, you're awake. Good, I'll bring you some tea.'

She jumped violently at the sound of his voice. He was standing at the foot of the bed, looking completely normal and dressed in a white towelling bathrobe. His dark hair was wet, as if he'd just got out of the shower.

Wildly she stared at him, pulling the duvet up under her chin.

'Are you OK?' he said. He'd been about to turn away but he paused now, staring curiously at her.

'Yes,' she said, her voice coming out as little more than a squeak. 'Yes, perfectly, thank you.'

'Oh,' he said, 'I just wondered. You seem a bit. . .oh, I don't know. . .' he shrugged '. . .not yourself somehow. Anyway, don't get up for a moment. I've made the tea; I won't be long.'

He wasn't long, but it was long enough for Kirstin to pull herself together and put some of the wilder possibilities out of her mind.

When he came back he set the tray down on a chest of drawers and poured the tea, then crossed to the bed and handed one mug to Kirstin, before perching on the side of the bed on the cream coloured duvet and proceeding to sip from his own mug.

Just like a married couple, she thought, then firmly dismissed the idea, not allowing it to develop any further.

'So, did you sleep?' he said at last, and again it was for all the world the sort of question that any husband might ask of his wife as they sipped early morning tea together in bed.

'Er, yes. Yes, thank you,' she said, then uncertainly she added, 'Did you?'

'Eventually,' he replied. 'But. . .you are OK?' He was staring at her again.

'I think so,' she replied, still in the same unnaturally high voice. 'But, I have to say, Harry. . .'

'Yes?' He turned his head to look at her. His bathrobe had fallen open to reveal a covering of dark hair on his chest and on his legs.

Hastily Kirstin looked away.

'Well. . .' she took a deep breath '. . .it isn't every day a girl wakes up in a strange bed and doesn't know how she got there.' Even to her, it sounded prim.

He frowned and took another mouthful of his tea.

'It isn't exactly a strange bed,' he said. 'It's my bed. And I would have thought it's pretty obvious how you got there.'

'It is?' It was Kirstin's turn to raise her eyebrows.

'Of course.' He paused. 'Well, how do you think you got there?'

'I really don't know, Harry. Maybe you should enlighten me. The last thing I recall I was sitting on the sofa with you. We'd both drunk some brandy and I was feeling very sleepy. . .'

'Yes,' he agreed, 'and I'd just kissed you.' He made it sound completely matter-of-fact, as if it was an everyday occurrence. 'You appeared to enjoy it—at least, you made no objection—then you promptly fell asleep.'

'Did I?' she stared doubtfully at him.

He nodded. 'You were tired, don't forget. No, more than that, I would say you were absolutely shattered. You'd had a very long day and you were completely drained, both physically and emotionally. . .'

'And I guess the brandy just about finished me off. . .'

'Exactly. Anyway, I waited a while but you showed no signs of waking up. On the contrary, you were in a very deep sleep. So deep that you hardly stirred when I brought you up here and put you to bed.'

'You carried me?' She stared at him.

'How else do you think you got up here?'

'Well, I. . .I don't know, really,' she said helplessly. 'And you say you put me to bed. . .' Her gaze flickered to her clothes on the chair.

'Yes, I took your suit off. You offered no resistance, I might add.' He gave a dry chuckle. 'Anyway, I thought you'd be more comfortable. And I didn't think you'd want your suit creased beyond all recognition, especially if you wanted to wear it to work today.

'Talking of work. . .' he drained his mug and stood up '. . .we'd better get a move on or we shall be late. Please, feel free to use the shower.'

'Harry.' She took another deep breath. Suddenly she had to know.

'Yes?' He paused and looked down at her.

'Where. . .?' She swallowed and tried again. 'Where exactly did you sleep?'

He stared at her, as if for a moment not quite understanding what she meant, and then, as his tawny gaze moved to the empty space beside her, he must have caught the drift of her question and quite suddenly a gleam of amusement entered his eyes.

'Where do you think I slept?' he said softly.

'Well, I hope it was on the sofa,' she replied.

'But you're not sure? Is that it?'

She nodded and, to her dismay, instead of answering her he began to untie his bathrobe.

'Harry. What are you doing?' she said sharply, her question forgotten now in the sudden possibility of this new, perhaps more worrying development.

'I told you,' he said calmly. 'We are going to be late. I've had my shower. I need to dress. If you wish to shower it is over there.' He pointed to the far side of the room.

She did want to shower. She wanted the loo as well

but, conscious of the fact that she was only wearing the briefest of briefs under her blouse, she had hoped that he was going to leave the room before she got out of bed.

That didn't now seem likely, however, and before she could think any further he had taken off the bathrobe completely and was standing with his back to her, completely naked.

In the moment before she slid out of bed and fled to the bathroom Kirstin was fleetingly aware of a muscular back, powerful shoulders and firm buttocks, and—as he half turned to her in apparent amusement—of a smattering of dark hair, a flat stomach and strong, lean thighs.

Then it was over and she was in the sanctuary of the bathroom. Leaning against the closed door, she took several deep breaths—glad to have escaped from his amused, slightly mocking smile.

The trouble was, she told herself a few moments later as she stepped into the shower, she was still none the wiser as to where he had spent the night.

By the time she cautiously returned to the bedroom it was empty.

When she peered over the spiral staircase she could see Harry in the room below. He was fully dressed now, and moving around between sitting-room and kitchen.

She picked up her jacket from the back of the chair and her case, which Harry presumably had brought up the night before, and went slowly, carefully, down the stairs, wondering as she did so how on earth he had managed to carry her up.

'Toast and coffee,' he said, appearing in the archway that led to the kitchen area.

'Oh, I think I should go home, really. I need to—'

'Toast and coffee,' he said again firmly and she realised that it had been a command, not an offer.

There wasn't time that morning to sit on the balcony, in spite of the fact that it was warm, bright and sunny.

And, in a way, Kirstin was glad there was no time to linger. She still felt embarrassed by what had happened and as she ate her breakfast and drank her coffee she found herself avoiding Harry's eye. She was only too aware that he still found the whole thing slightly amusing, but somehow that only added to her sense of discomfort.

She made her escape soon after that and fled to her own apartment, where she changed her clothes, applied the light make-up she wore for work and brushed her hair.

By the time she reached the car park Harry had already left for work.

Hopefully, Kirstin thought as she got into her own car and drove to the centre, the incident would be forgotten and Harry would not refer to it again.

And although in the days that followed that was what happened, Kirstin was only too aware that something had changed between them and the balance of their relationship had again shifted.

She was unable to get that night out of her mind; found herself going over and over the events in her head, wondering anew if he had, in fact, slept beside her, and countless times reliving the moment when he had kissed her.

The days slipped by, as frantic, as busy, as ever. Charles Hardiman's funeral took place and the centre closed for a couple of hours to give the staff a chance to pay their last respects and say goodbye to the senior partner they had all loved.

The church in the heart of Maybury was packed with relatives, friends and patients, an indication to all of just how much this man had meant to the community.

At the graveside in the cemetery—in the company of the other partners—Kirstin found herself watching Juliet, cool and elegant in black, as she comforted Estelle. The tall man at Juliet's side, Kirstin guessed, was her husband, Paul, and the small boy who threw a rose into the open grave their son, Matthew. Their grief was contagious and when at last they all turned from the grave it was the sound of Eva, weeping noisily, that filled the summer afternoon.

Kirstin's undoing came when she was walking the gravel path beneath the yews to the road and, glancing at Harry who walked beside her, she saw tears rolling unchecked down his rugged features.

Quietly, without hesitation, she slipped her hand in his and squeezed it.

He, in turn, gripped hers tightly and continued to hold it until they reached the row of parked cars.

They couldn't all go back to Fir Tree Lodge as there were surgeries to take so, when Estelle asked who could come, Bruce—quickly for him—decided that Harry, Isabella and Eva should go so that all sections of the staff were represented.

'And Kirstin,' said Harry quietly. 'I want Kirstin to go.'

'Very well,' Bruce said, no doubt from past experience recognising the tone of his partner's voice as one there was no point arguing with, 'Kirstin as well.'

She was suddenly, ridiculously pleased—and surprised, too—that Harry should have asked that she go.

Harry must have picked up on this element of surprise as he took his place beside her in the Citroën and they drove away from the cemetery.

'He would have wanted it,' he said simply. 'He was fond of you, Kirstin.'

She nodded, not trusting herself to speak—afraid that she would be unable to negotiate the lump in her throat.

A cold buffet was set out in the dining-room of Fir Tree Lodge but the mourners soon wandered into the drawing-room and through the French doors into the grounds.

The gardens, Estelle's pride and joy, were particularly beautiful at that time of the year. The air was thick with the scent of roses, while clematis and wisteria tumbled from trellis archways and red hot pokers gleamed from the misty blue depths of the deep herbaceous borders.

Kirstin, clutching a glass of the excellent cream sherry that Charles had always kept, stood on the terrace admiring the scene.

'I wonder if she'll stay here now Charles has gone,' murmured a voice at her elbow.

Turning, Kirstin found Isabella beside her. 'I don't know,' she replied, 'but I would like to think that she could, if that is what she wants.'

'I was watching those two over there.' Isabella nodded towards a far corner of the garden.

When Kirstin turned she saw, with a sudden pang, Harry and Juliet, standing together beneath the golden cascade of a laburnum tree. It reminded Kirstin of the time she had found them in the hallway of this very house when she and Harry had visited Charles on his discharge from hospital. They had been deep in conversation then, their heads close together, just as they were now.

'Makes you wonder, doesn't it?' said Isabella softly.

'Wonder what?' Kirstin threw her a sidelong glance.

'If the rumours were true. If it was her he was engaged to all those years ago. If she was the one he hasn't been able to get over.'

Kirstin didn't answer. She didn't want to confirm that she knew for a fact that it had, indeed, been Juliet to whom Harry had been engaged, and for some reason she certainly didn't want the old rumours started again about him not being able to get over his love.

Why she felt that way, she didn't know; she wasn't even sure what it was she felt as she continued to watch the couple beneath the laburnum. She only knew that it hurt.

'I suppose I should be getting back,' said Isabella with a sigh. 'I have a baby clinic this afternoon.'

'Yes, I expect we'll be leaving soon as well,' said Kirstin, glancing across the lawn towards Harry again.

'If Harry can drag himself away,' said Isabella drily as she turned to go back into the house. 'I must go and find Estelle,' she added.

Kirstin would have joined her—anything to get away from the scene that was causing her pain—but as she turned to go she caught sight of Juliet's husband, Paul. He was standing on the far side of the terrace, a glass in his hand, and he, too, was watching Juliet and Harry.

She wondered what he was thinking. He also must have known about their past relationship. Did he ever wonder if they still meant anything to each other? Was he, too, feeling pain? After all, he must love Juliet.

The sudden logic behind her thoughts hit Kirstin like a bolt from the blue. If Paul was feeling pain because he loved Juliet why should she, Kirstin, be feeling pain?

The answer was suddenly only too clear. Her pain was caused by jealousy, and her jealousy was because she was in love.

But how could that be? She didn't even like Harry Brolin. So how could she be in love with him?

He looked up then and saw her. He said something to Juliet, touched her arm and kissed her briefly on the cheek.

To Kirstin, watching him and waiting for him, the action only intensified her curiosity as to whether the rumours were true—whether Harry Brolin really was a one-woman man and would remain so for ever.

He walked away from Juliet, leaving her in the shade of the laburnum, crossed the lawn and ran up the short flight of stone steps to the terrace where he nodded briefly to Paul.

'We'd best be going,' he said abruptly to Kirstin when Paul barely acknowledged him. 'We have a couple of house calls to make before we go back to the surgery. Let's find Estelle.'

She nodded and with one last glance at Juliet and then at Paul—who had continued to stand, perfectly still, watching his wife—she turned and followed Harry into the house.

They were closer after the day of the funeral but there were no more moments of shared intimacy and for Kirstin, now that she had recognised the fact that she loved him, their relationship became bitter-sweet.

Time and again in the weeks that followed Charles's death she was tempted to tell Harry how she felt—this was the 1990s, for heaven's sake, not the 1890s—but always something stopped her.

Gradually she came to understand that it was the fear of the rumour about him being correct that prevented her from revealing her feelings. If the rumour was correct and Harry, indeed, did not want any other woman but Juliet then she knew that she faced certain rejection, and Kirstin wasn't sure she was ready for that.

One day maybe, one day it might be inevitable, but not just yet.

For the time being she would simply enjoy living and working in close proximity to the man she loved, and at the same time continue to marvel at how the tables had been turned and how utter dislike had turned to love.

It might have continued like that for the remainder of Kirstin's year at Maybury, but she was never to know because one fateful day in the heat of the summer everything changed.

*   *   *

It began with the arrival of a letter for Kirstin. The letter had been forwarded by her mother and bore a New Zealand stamp.

'It must be from Scott,' her mother wrote in the accompanying letter, 'so I'm sending it on to you straight away. You must be longing to hear from him after all this time.'

Kirstin had to quell a stab of guilt as she slit the back of the envelope and withdrew the letter. She had hardly thought of Scott at all in the last few weeks.

She read the letter through once quickly, then had to sit down and read it again more slowly.

Scott had met someone else—a New Zealand girl who had recently joined the crew. It had, apparently, been love at first sight for them both and they wanted to marry. Scott had written:

> I really didn't know how to tell you because, although we had never really talked of marriage, I felt the possibility was always there—probably coming more from our parents than from us. I do love you Kirstin. I always have, since we were very small, and I guess I always will but, I'm sorry, what I feel for you is not the same as I feel for Helen. I do hope you will understand and that you may even be able to feel happy for me.

'Oh, I do. I do,' she whispered, staring at the letter through a blur of tears. At one time she might have thought it acceptable if she and Scott had drifted into marriage. Now, she knew otherwise.

Kirstin felt no jealousy, no animosity, towards the unknown Helen; she just hoped that she would make Scott happy.

If only it could happen that way for her.

Ruefully she folded the letter and put it back in its envelope.

But there seemed little chance of that. Harry hardly seemed to know she existed—at least, not in that way.

She spent the best part of that particular afternoon assisting Rhannie and Val with a baby clinic then, as the day drew to a close, she went into Reception. Eva had just informed her that Mrs Selby had gone into hospital that day for her hysterectomy when suddenly Harry practically erupted from his room.

'Where's the fire?' Kirstin joked.

'Parkside Estate,' he replied abruptly, 'and it isn't a fire, it's a baby. Home confinement—possible complications,' he shouted over his shoulder.

'Can I come?' she called back.

'If you like. Could be a long job. Best bring your car and follow me.'

'OK.' She shrugged helplessly at Eva and dashed out of the building after Harry.

It wasn't until she got into her car in the compound that Kirstin realised that her medical case was in her consulting-room. She wanted to go back for it but didn't dare ask Harry to wait. On the other hand, she didn't want him to go without her because she knew that if she couldn't follow him she would be sure to lose her way in the maze of streets on the Parkside Estate.

In the end, coming to a rapid decision, she reluctantly decided to leave her bag. Harry would have all they would be likely to need in his own bag. It was far more important that they should get to the patient on time.

With the sudden rush of adrenalin which was becoming more and more familiar these days whenever she accompanied Harry, Kirstin started her car and, following him, drove out of the compound.

CHAPTER ELEVEN

KIRSTIN lost Harry once in the heavy rush-hour traffic around Maybury but luckily caught sight of the dark blue Citroën on the roundabout exit to Parkside.

By the time she arrived at the house his car was parked outside and Harry had gone in.

A crowd of children were grouped around the gate. One, a little girl, was swinging on the bars while another, probably even younger, bounced up and down on an already partly demolished hedge.

They stared with interest at Kirstin as she got out of her car. Carefully she locked it with a silent prayer that it would still be there and in the same condition when she returned.

'Are you the police?' asked another child, a taller boy with red hair. He said it quite matter-of-factly.

'No,' said Kirstin, 'I'm a doctor.'

'Doctor's already gone in,' said the boy, suspicious now.

'I know,' said Kirstin, walking right up to the gate, angry for feeling nervous. They were only children, after all, she told herself firmly. 'That was Dr Brolin. I'm Dr Patterson—we work together.'

'Has your mum had her baby yet?' Another of the group, an older girl, looked at the boy with red hair who sniffed then shook his head.

'Nah, not yet,' he said.

'Is your dad around?' asked Kirstin, looking up at the house.

'Me dad?' the boy stared at her. 'Oh, you mean Terry?

158

He's not our dad. He's upstairs with Mam—oh, no, there he is. . .'

The front door had opened and, looking up quickly, Kirstin saw a young man dressed in jeans and a grubby white T-shirt. His dark hair was long and greasy and there was at least three days' stubble on his chin.

'You the other doc?' he called when he caught sight of Kirstin.

'Yes.' She swallowed. 'Can I come in?'

'S'pose so.' He stood aside for her to enter the house. 'Can't see what she wants two doctors for,' he muttered. 'Not as if it's her first.'

Kirstin didn't answer. Instead, as he nodded up the stairs, she squeezed past him in the narrow hallway.

'Front bedroom,' he said.

When she was halfway up the stairs and just before he shut the front door she hear him say to the children, 'Clear off you lot—you'll only be in the way. I'll tell you when you can come back.'

She hurried on to the bedroom, tapped on the door and pushed it open.

The patient was probably in her late twenties but with her thin face and long fair hair she didn't look much older than some of the children who had been playing outside.

The midwife, Caroline Marshall, was talking to Harry who had removed his jacket, and was standing by the window rolling up his shirtsleeves.

He looked up as Kirstin came into the room. 'What kept you?' he said.

At one time that would have worried Kirstin but by now she knew Harry well enough to know that it was said with a touch of humour.

'This is Marissa,' he said looking down at the woman on the bed.

'Hello, Marissa,' she smiled, and the woman managed

a weak smile in response. Kirstin then nodded at the midwife whom she had already met on previous occasions.

'This is Marissa's fourth baby,' said Harry, 'but it appears to be showing a bit of reluctance over putting in an appearance.'

Kirstin found herself thinking that she didn't really blame it under the circumstances, then she dismissed the thought. It wasn't her place to sit in any kind of judgement. Instead, she looked at Harry and said, 'Do we know what the problem is?'

He nodded but it was Caroline Marshall who explained.

'We have a "face to pubes" delivery here,' she said. 'It's taking a very long time, as they usually do, and Marissa is getting very tired. I've explained that we may have to get her into hospital for a forceps delivery but she's not at all happy with that idea. I kept hoping that baby would turn and change its position, but I don't think there's much chance of that now.'

'How much is she dilated?' asked Harry.

'Nearly eight centimetres.'

'I'd better take a look.' Harry opened his case.

Kirstin sat down beside Marissa and after a moment she said, 'I believe I saw your other children outside.' Suddenly she felt sorry for the young woman on the bed who, if anything, was probably younger than herself. 'You have three, don't you?' she added conversationally.

'Yes,' Marissa replied through gritted teeth. 'A boy, Rory. . .and two girls, Amber and Tania. . .' She gasped as another contraction seized her thin body and grabbed hold of Kirstin's hand. 'Oh, why doesn't it come?' she wailed. 'The others didn't take this long. . .!'

'The foetal heart is fine,' Harry murmured to Caroline a few moments later after he'd examined Marissa. Then, turning back to Marissa, he said cheerfully, 'Baby has a nice strong heartbeat.'

For one moment Kirstin thought that Marissa was going to hit him.

The labour progressed slowly. Terry, at Caroline's request—but rather grudgingly, Kirstin thought— brought them tea, but it was late evening and just when Harry was on the point of suggesting a transfer to hospital that Caroline announced that the cervix was now ten centimetres dilated and that she could feel the anterior fontanelle.

'Baby's nearly here,' said Kirstin encouragingly, lifting the gas and air mask from Marissa's face. But the poor woman was so exhausted by this time that Harry's concern was that she wouldn't have enough strength left to get through the second stage of labour.

'I want Terry,' Marissa sobbed as yet another contraction subsided.

Until then Terry had alternated between hovering in the doorway and running up and down the stairs fetching and carrying or yelling at the children.

Now, when Caroline told him what Marissa wanted, he came dubiously into the bedroom and sat down beside her, taking her other hand. His presence seemed to rally Marissa and from somewhere she found the extra strength needed to push.

As the baby's head finally crowned Harry instructed Kirstin to draw up an injection of Synometrine to prevent the risk of a haemorrhage in the final stage of labour.

The child was born with its tiny face upwards, as Caroline had predicted, and as one shoulder appeared Kirstin administered the injection.

'It's a girl,' said Caroline, lifting the baby onto Marissa's chest. 'A fine healthy girl, by the looks of it, even if she was a bit lazy about making her entrance.'

'Well done, Marissa,' said Kirstin, squeezing the mother's hand. 'She's beautiful.'

Marissa was smiling now and even the sullen-faced Terry had tears running down his cheeks as he gazed at the baby.

Glancing up, Kirstin's eyes met Harry's and if she had previously been in any doubt it was in that moment— as he stood at the foot of the bed in his shirtsleeves, his hair dishevelled, with blood on his hands and with a silly grin on his face as they shared that moment of pure joy— that Kirstin knew that she loved him.

'It's a miracle,' he said his voice husky and catching in his throat. 'Every time I see it I still think it.'

'Are you going to deliver this placenta or am I, Dr Brolin?' asked Caroline coolly.

'Sorry, Sister.' Harry pulled a face and they all laughed, relieving the emotion and tension in the room. 'I'll do it; finish the job properly,' he said, then added, 'And then I suggest we let those children see their new sister. I can't imagine any of them are going to go to sleep until they do.'

'I don't know about you,' he said half an hour later as they left the house, 'but I could do with a drink. If we're quick we should just about catch one of the pubs before they close.'

'You're on,' said Kirstin wearily, climbing into her car.

She followed his car to The Britannia, an off-the-street pub in downtown Maybury.

'Not the sort of place you would normally frequent,' he commented with a smile as he bought her a drink.

'Probably not,' she admitted, glancing round, 'but I'm getting used to these new experiences—like sitting at the bar and not at a table.' She grinned at him.

'So you think you're getting everything sussed out now, do you?' Harry picked up the two glasses and, after speaking to the barman who seemed to know him well, handed one to Kirstin then took a long draught of his beer.

'I needed that,' he said, setting the glass down on the bar and half turning towards her.

'Yes,' she said slowly, 'I do believe at last I'm beginning to suss things out. Maybury, the practice, and the people. . .'

'Good,' he said, 'I'm glad to hear it.' Then, casually, he went on, 'So what did you make of that set-up tonight?'

'What do you mean?' She frowned.

'Well, from your expression once or twice there, I gather you didn't really approve of young Terry.'

'It wasn't for me to approve or disapprove,' she said firmly, 'and I certainly hope I didn't—'

'Oh, come on, Kirstin,' he chuckled. 'It was obvious, and Terry knew it—that's why he was so wary.'

Kirstin was silent for a moment, smarting under a criticism she considered to be unjust, then—quietly controlling her anger—she said, 'I just happen to think it's a shame, that's all.'

'That what's a shame?' He raised one eyebrow and looked at her.

'Those sort of situations,' she replied carefully. 'There are so many these days.'

'Really?' he said softly, the tawny eyes suddenly opaque. 'Exactly what sort of situations did you mean?'

'Oh, for goodness' sake, Harry—' she was irritated now '—surely you don't need me to spell it out.'

'Actually, yes, I do. I do need you to spell it out,' he said in the same soft tones, 'because I think you might be mistaken; might be jumping to conclusions, as so many people do. . .'

'Oh, I don't think so.' She set her glass down onto the bar with a thump which made the barman look in their direction. But she didn't care. She was really angry

now. How dared he try to tell her that she was jumping
to conclusions when the whole thing was perfectly clear
for anyone with an atom of insight to see?

'For a start,' she said, 'Terry wasn't the children's
father. The older child, Rory, confirmed that.' Then,
goaded by some inner demon, she swept irrationally on,
'And that's another thing. Rory had flaming red hair,
which the girls didn't and Marissa certainly didn't so
there could well have been more than one other man
involved. And now I would say this Terry has moved in
and fathered yet another child. . . It's irresponsible, that's
what it is. . .'

'So, that's what you think, is it?' Harry was watching
her closely and when she didn't reply he went on, but
now his voice had an unfamiliar edge to it. 'Just when
I thought you might be beginning to settle down you start
making wild assumptions, based on pure speculation.'

'What do you mean?' Kirstin stared at him, hardly
able to believe what she was hearing.

'What I say,' he replied shortly. 'You're quite wrong,
you know, about Marissa.'

'Oh, I am, am I?' she retorted. 'Well, I'm sure you're
about to enlighten me.'

'You've already decided Terry is a no-good,
haven't you?'

'I would say that's probably a fair assumption. . .'

'So, what would you say if I was to tell you that he's
probably the best thing that's happened to Marissa?'

'Well, if he's the best then I shudder to think what the
other things were. . .' she exploded.

'Yes, Kirstin, you would,' he said, his voice soft again
now. 'Shudder, that is. She comes,' he went on when
Kirstin stiffened, 'from an appalling background of abuse
and neglect.'

'What do you mean. . .?'

'She had Rory when she was only fifteen,' he said

quietly, 'the result of a rape by a member of her family. Her husband was a hopeless no-good who never worked and squandered his benefits on drink. He's in prison now for armed robbery.'

He stared into the bottom of his glass for a long moment then said, 'Terry, on the other hand, comes from a good home. He's known Marissa since they were children.'

'But the baby. . .?' said Kirstin. 'What about the baby?'

'It isn't Terry's.' Harry shook his head. 'It's her husband's. Conceived on the night he beat Marissa up so badly she landed up in hospital. Terry has cared for her and the children ever since, just as I dare say he'll go on doing. . . Shall I go on?' he asked, without looking up.

Kirstin remained silent, not knowing what to say. She was appalled that she could have been so wrong.

'So you see,' said Harry a moment later as he drained his glass, 'you really can't allow yourself to jump to any conclusions until you know the facts. Things are never quite what they seem, Kirstin. Now, if you've finished, I suggest we get home.'

The evening was ruined. That moment of sheer joy they had shared—a moment when Kirstin could briefly have believed he might feel something for her—had gone, probably for ever, never to be repeated.

She followed him despondently out of the pub, deliberately sitting for a moment in her car and watching as he drove away.

She knew the way back to the docks from here and wouldn't need to follow him quite so closely. But she had another reason for lingering. She wanted to call in at the centre and collect her medical case. Harry hadn't appeared to notice that she didn't have it with her. She hadn't dared to tell him that she'd left it behind, and that had been before he'd been so annoyed with her. Heaven only knew what his reaction would have been now.

There was very little traffic about and as Kirstin approached the centre she glanced at the digital clock on her dashboard and saw that it was 11.40 p.m.

She knew that really she should unlock the compound and park her car in there, but she also knew that what she had to do would only take a few minutes.

On a sudden impulse she decided to park on the forecourt.

She had her own set of keys for the centre but, knowing what a performance it was to unlock the iron grille and then the mortice locks on the front door, she went to the rear of the building and the staff door.

While this door had as many locks it had no iron grille so the exercise should be quicker and easier.

As she approached the door, however, an overhead security light suddenly came on and made her jump. She knew the lights were there, of course, but had quite forgotten them.

Muttering to herself that she was glad she wasn't in the burglary business, Kirstin unlocked the door and let herself into the building.

It was pitch dark inside.

She fumbled, found the light switch then turned and carefully locked the door behind her. It wouldn't do to let someone into the building while she was inside.

The door opened into a narrow passage at the very rear of the building, with storerooms and a cloakroom leading off it.

Taking a deep breath, Kirstin hurried along the passage towards the room she had been using to take her surgeries.

The empty building seemed eerie and alien at night without the noise and bustle of the daytime—the clamour of patients, the chatter of the staff and the constantly ringing telephones. Kirstin decided that she didn't like it much and would get out as fast as she could.

As she turned the corner of the passage she saw a dim glow ahead.

What on earth was it?

Then she remembered—it was the security light that burned all night in Reception.

She had almost reached her room when she thought she heard a faint sound.

She froze and listened.

All was silent. She wasn't even sure where the sound had come from. Maybe one of the other doctors had come in for some notes, or perhaps someone was working late. But that seemed unlikely, especially at this time of night. It was Harry who was on call and Kirstin was pretty certain that he hadn't come here.

Maybe she should investigate? But she wasn't sure that she was brave enough for that.

But supposing someone had seen her park and come into the centre and even now was vandalising her car? Supposing that had been the noise she had heard?

Incensed by the thought, she crept forward into Reception. From there she could see out of the window onto the forecourt. If there was someone there she could phone the police.

Reception was dim and shadowy, the computers shrouded and the phones silent.

Kirstin found herself wishing that Eva was there then, if there were any vandals, she wouldn't need to phone the police—one glimpse of big Eva in full cry would be enough to thwart the most hardened of criminals.

Her heart pounding, she lifted one corner of the Venetian blind and peered out.

Her car was just where she had left it. She could see it quite clearly in the light from an overhead streetlamp outside the centre. All was quiet and there was no one around. With a sigh of relief Kirstin let the blind go.

She had begun to wish that she hadn't come in; had taken a chance and left her case, hoping that Harry wouldn't find out and deliver a sermon.

Now, all she wanted was to collect the offending object and get out of this place.

The centre was not the most pleasant of buildings, even during the day, thought Kirstin as she hurried back down the passage to the consulting-rooms, and at night it was the stuff nightmares were made of.

She didn't even pause this time when she reached her door, just wrenched the handle and, pushing it open, strode into the room and flicked the light switch.

Afterwards, when she thought about it and was able to remember it, she wasn't sure who'd been the more surprised as she'd stood there frozen to the spot—she or the man in the Balaclava, crouched in front of the cupboard in the corner of her room. Transfixed in the sudden light, his wild eyes had stared back at her from the gap in the knitted black wool.

A second later Kirstin had reeled from a blow to the back of her neck, then the world had spun away out of her control as everything went black.

Someone was stroking her forehead. It was soothing and very, very pleasant. Content to let it be, she drifted back to sleep.

This time someone was holding her hand, gently squeezing it then releasing it.

Someone was talking; her father's voice, surely.

But that couldn't be. He wasn't here, he was at home.

Again she was too tired to think about it. Again she slipped back into the safe cocoon of sleep.

Then it was light. A brightness that hurt even through her closed eyelids.

Hurt even more when she opened them.

But that was nothing, compared to the pain in her head when she moved.

She remained still for a long time until the pain subsided, peering through half-closed eyes. The world seemed fuzzy, like an out-of-focus photograph. There were objects, white objects, moving around.

She moved her head again and this time it hurt less, only slightly so but the pain was at least bearable.

Slowly, very slowly, she moved, an inch at a time to prevent sudden jarring.

To her surprise she was in a bed with her head supported by many pillows, and sitting beside her was the figure of a man. His shoulders were hunched, his head supported by one hand. With a slightly unreal sense of wonder Kirstin realised that his other hand was covering hers where it lay on a green and yellow striped bedspread.

'Harry. . .?' Her voice was little more than a choked whisper.

Common sense told her that it couldn't be Harry. Harry had gone home.

He lifted his head sharply and stared at her.

It was Harry.

Kirstin felt tears ooze from under her eyelids and roll down her face. She was too tired to even wipe them away.

'Kirstin?' he said softly then, leaning forward, he scrutinised her face, his eyes full of concern.

To Kirstin, watching, there was something else besides concern in his eyes, but at that moment she couldn't for the life of her think what it was.

Harry,' she said weakly. 'What happened? Whatever happened? Where am I?'

'Whoa,' he said shakily, the emotion in his voice only too apparent now. 'One question at a time. You are in Maybury City General.' He paused and asked, 'Do you remember anything of what happened?'

She frowned, afraid that the concentration of thinking was going to prove too much; that once again she was going to slip back into that place of soft dark oblivion, but at the same time knowing that if she did it would be happily—simply because Harry was with her.

'I went back to the centre,' she said slowly and with great effort at last. 'To get my case. . .' she added.

He nodded. 'We thought that,' he said.

'I don't know what happened. . .I parked on the fore-court because I thought I wouldn't be long. . . It was very dark. . . I went in the back door. . .' She trailed off, trying to clear the fog from her mind.

'Yes,' prompted Harry gently when it seemed that she might be unable to continue, 'you went in the back door. What did you do then?'

'I don't know. . .' She hesitated. 'I can't remember. . .' Her voice rose slightly, taking on an edge of panic.

'It's OK,' said Harry easily. 'It doesn't matter.'

'But how did I get here?' She frowned. 'Why am I here? Why does my head hurt so much?'

'You disturbed intruders at the centre,' said Harry.

Leaning across the bedspread, he took her other hand and held both tightly while Kirstin gazed at him in fear.

'They were in your room,' he said. 'They'd already ransacked the safe in the office. Then they broke into your cupboard and found your case, which Eva had locked away. They'd taken the drugs and your prescription pads.'

'So what happened. . .when I. . .?'

'They clocked you one.' He spoke casually, but the underlying anxiety and anger in his tone was obvious. 'They hit you across the back of the head, Kirstin. You have a fractured skull.'

She raised her head and stared at him for a long moment, then lay back on her pillows. 'That accounts for the headache,' she said weakly.

'You've had severe concussion. . .'

'But how did you know. . .? You'd gone home. . . When we left the pub you went home. . .'

'I was worried about you,' he said.

'You were?' She stared at him. This concern was definitely something new.

'Yes, I'd had a go at you in the pub and I was feeling guilty.'

Her amazement must have shown for he gave a rueful smile. 'Seems unlikely, I know, but there it was. Anyway, it was a good thing because I decided to wait for you when I got back to The Warehouse and apologise. When you didn't arrive I became concerned. I thought you might have had an accident or your car might have broken down or something, so I went back to look for you. I went all the way to the pub but there was no sign of you. Then something, God knows what, told me to try the centre.'

He paused and Kirstin saw the tawny eyes darken.

'I saw your car on the forecourt,' he went on after a while, 'then, when I let myself in, I found you unconscious in your room.'

He stopped, as if struggling to overcome his emotion, then he said, 'You still don't remember anything?'

'No,' she said slowly, 'nothing after going in through the back door. . . At least. . .' She trailed off, frowning deeply again.

'Perhaps it's just as well,' said Harry. 'You've had us all worried, though, I can tell you that. . . Your parents have been beside themselves—'

'My parents? How did they know?' She stared at him in fresh amazement.

'I phoned them soon after it had happened. They came up straight away—'

'You mean they are here?' Her eyes widened in disbelief.

'Yes.' Harry nodded.

So it had been her father's voice she'd heard. She hadn't dreamt it or imagined it.

'I just persuaded them to get some rest,' Harry went on after a moment. 'They've been with you all the time. I said I would take their place for a while.'

'So, how long have I been here, for heaven's sake?'

'This is the third day,' said Harry quietly. 'You were unconscious for two days, and today you've been drifting in and out.'

She continued to stare helplessly at him, unable to take in what he had said, then she closed her eyes. 'I thought it was only last night it happened,' she said at last.

She slept again after that, but it was a more peaceful sleep. When she awoke again, although Harry had gone and her mother was by her side, the first thing that Kirstin remembered was the look that had been in Harry's eyes the last time she had woken up.

He came to see her as often as he could and even brought flowers once, an air of embarrassment about him as he set them on her bed.

It was decided that she was to stay in hospital under observation for a further week. Eventually, when she was out of danger, her parents returned home.

'But I shall be back to get you when you are discharged,' her father said firmly on the morning they left.

'I'm sure there's no need, Daddy,' she protested, still too weak to offer much resistance.

'Nonsense,' her father replied. 'You are coming home to recuperate and that's that.'

She didn't have the strength to argue further. And it would be nice to see the Island again, especially in high summer, even though secretly she would have preferred to stay in Maybury—to return quietly to The Warehouse and let Harry take care of her.

But that, she knew, would hardly be fair. For one thing he was far too busy, and for another he hadn't offered to do so; hadn't even indicated that he would be prepared to as much as watch out for her.

Her hospital room began to resemble a florist's as flowers arrived from friends at home and from colleagues at the centre.

Then, as word got round, cards began to arrive with every delivery of post. Many of the cards were from patients who had heard of the attack on their new doctor, and who wanted to show their outrage at what had happened and at the same time express their feelings towards her.

Kirstin was deeply touched and overwhelmed by people's kindness. She attempted to say as much to Isabella when she visited.

'You're popular. They like you,' said Isabella simply.

'I didn't think they'd even noticed me,' said Kirstin, once again fighting the tears that now always seemed to be near the surface. 'I thought I was simply another doctor—that it didn't really matter who they saw. . .'

'That may be the case with some doctors,' said Isabella, 'and likewise with some of the people, but sometimes a doctor comes along who develops a rapport with the people. Harry Brolin has that rapport—they like and respect him, just as they did Dr Hardiman—and now you seem to have achieved the same thing.'

'So much so that they bash me over the head.' Kirstin managed a wry smile.

'Ah, well,' replied Isabella quickly, 'that's another thing—they've caught the pair responsible. Anonymous tip-off, apparently—at least, according to Hayley who has contacts about these things.'

'Really?' Kirstin stared at her in amazement. 'But why should anyone do that? Give a tip-off, I mean?'

'I told you—you've become well liked around here.'

Isabella's dark eyes flashed wickedly. 'And you'd better hurry up and come back—Harry's like a bear with a sore head without you.'

'Don't be silly. . .' Kirstin protested. She had no difficulty in imagining Harry behaving like a bear with a sore head. What was harder was believing that it had anything to do with her absence.

'You think I'm joking?' Isabella looked surprised. 'It's true. Ask any of the others. Even Val said as much today and that's saying something, I can tell you. For her to admit that Harry is actually pining for another woman. Well!' She grinned. 'Seriously, Kirstin, I would say you've got our Dr Brolin quite smitten.'

After Isabella had gone Kirstin lay and thought over all she'd said and gradually it all began to make a crazy sort of sense.

There had been a change in Harry's attitude towards her, she knew that—the look that had been in his eyes when she'd come round, the fact that he had waited for her that night to apologise for upsetting her and then the fact that he had gone to look for her because he was worried about her.

And now there was Isabella, telling her that he was missing her.

Did it, could it, all add up to something?

Could it possibly, even remotely, suggest that he was beginning to feel for her what she did for him?

Kirstin wasn't sure. All she did know was that now she had cause to hope.

And then, on the day she was to be discharged from the hospital—while she was waiting for her father to drive up from Portsmouth to collect her—she had a visit from Estelle, and quietly her world fell apart.

CHAPTER TWELVE

THE visit started happily enough with Estelle, in a pretty floral dress and laden with yet more flowers, coming into the room and smiling warmly at Kirstin. 'I'm sorry I haven't managed to get in to see you before,' she said. 'And now they tell me you are going home later today.'

'That's right.' Kirstin smiled. 'Everyone is insisting I go to the Island to recuperate. I've given up arguing about it.'

'Quite right, too,' said Estelle firmly. 'That was a nasty experience you had, Kirstin. I only hope it hasn't put you off us all.'

'Of course it hasn't.' Kirstin glanced round at all the cards and flowers. 'How could it, especially when everyone's been so kind? Anyway, that's quite enough about me; how are you now?' She threw Estelle a keen glance and noticed that, although the older woman still looked thin and rather drawn, she was looking slightly better than on the last occasion Kirstin had seen her.

'I think I'm starting to come to terms with losing Charles.' Estelle gave a little sigh. 'Oh, I know it's going to take a long time—after all, we were married for nearly forty years—but it's very true what people say about life going on. It does, you know. . .' she paused '. . .and you have to let it.'

'Yes, I suppose you do. I'm not sure how I'd cope, though,' said Kirstin dubiously.

'Family and friends are a great help.'

'Yes, I'm sure they are.' She paused, found herself hesitating, before saying, 'It must have been a great help having Juliet with you at the time.'

'It was,' Estelle agreed, 'and it still is.'

Kirstin frowned. 'You mean she's still with you?'

Estelle nodded. 'Yes, there didn't seem a lot of point in her going back to Oxford, especially now that Matthew is in boarding school.'

'But what about Paul, her husband?' asked Kirstin. 'Where is he?'

'Oh, he's still in Oxford.' Estelle leaned forward and smelt one of the yellow carnations that Harry had brought. 'Aren't they lovely?' she said.

Kirstin nodded absent-mindedly. 'Doesn't he mind that?' she asked curiously. 'Him being in Oxford, I mean, and his wife here in Maybury?'

Estelle straightened up and looked at her. 'He might have done once,' she said quietly, 'but I doubt it bothers him now that he and Juliet are separated.'

In the silence that followed Kirstin stared at her.

'Didn't you know?' asked Estelle.

'No,' she replied slowly, 'I didn't. I. . .I'm very sorry.'

'I suppose I'm getting used to it now.' Estelle sighed again. 'It's another one of those things that you know you just have to come to terms with. Charles was very upset about it.'

'You mean he knew?'

'Oh, gracious, yes,' said Estelle. 'It happened well over a year ago now.'

Kirstin stared at her in open amazement. 'A year ago? But. . .but I thought. . .'

'You thought they were still a couple?' Estelle raised an eyebrow.

'Well, yes, I suppose I did,' she replied slowly. 'That night when Charles had his stroke it was Paul who brought Juliet to the hospital, and then at the funeral he was there and he seemed. . .she seemed. . .oh, I don't know. . .' She trailed off uncomfortably as somewhere in the back of her mind a niggle had begun to form.

'Paul and Juliet have remained friends,' said Estelle, 'and I'm glad they have, for Matthew's sake. Paul was also very fond of Charles so it was understandable that he should want to help and to attend his funeral. Paul was still technically our son-in-law. . .and will be, I suppose, until after the divorce.'

'They're getting divorced?' Kirstin swallowed. The niggle was growing, threatening to turn into something unmanageable.

'Oh, yes.' Estelle sounded quite matter-of-fact about it then, leaning forward slightly again and lowering her voice, she said, 'Really, you know, Kirstin, they should never have got married in the first place.'

'Really?' Kirstin's voice sounded high, unnatural even to herself.

'I knew it wouldn't last,' Estelle went on. A faraway look had come into her eyes as if she had slipped back and was reliving some period of time in the past. 'Charles was ready to give them the benefit of the doubt, but I knew. I think we women do know these things.'

'Why didn't you think it would last?' asked Kirstin. She knew what she was going to hear; didn't really want it put into words, but some perversity egged her on.

'Because of Harry,' said Estelle. When Kirstin remained silent she went on, 'Juliet was in love with him really, you know. Oh, she allowed herself to become infatuated with Paul, but it was Harry she loved. From the moment she set eyes on him she loved him and, of course, he loved her. Still does, if I know anything about it. You can see it even now when they are together. He follows her with his eyes. . .'

She paused for a long moment and went on, 'Like I say, she should have married him in the first place. Still, it looks as if it might be a case of better late than never.'

There was a silence in the room, then carefully Kirstin

said, 'You think they will get together again—Harry and Juliet?'

'I don't doubt it,' said Estelle. 'After all, when the divorce comes through there'll be nothing to stop them.'

Her world had started to crumble when the niggle of suspicion had formed at the back of her mind. Now, finally, it fell apart.

How could she have been so wrong? How could she have thought that he cared? What she had thought might be the beginnings of love had, after all, only been the natural concern anyone would have shown towards a trainee or a colleague.

It was early evening. The beach was deserted, save for two men in the distance digging for bait, and the tide was going out to leave acres of wet sand and seaweed-strewn rock pools.

Kirstin walked across the loose dry sand, still warm from the day's sun, and onto the vast expanse of firmer sand washed by the tide. Her canvas shoes left imprints that quickly disappeared as she walked and a soft breeze from the sea stirred her hair, lifting strands and blowing them around her face.

She had been home for a week.

Physically she had recovered.

Emotionally she doubted she ever would.

Two days previously she had reached her decision and had written two letters, one to Bruce and one to Harry. The letters were practically identical, telling of her decision not to return to Maybury.

'I'm relieved, darling,' her mother had said, 'and I'm sure everyone will understand. It really isn't any wonder you don't want to go back there. I'm sure Hamish Forbes will find somewhere else for you to finish your training.'

'Yes, I dare say he will,' she'd replied.

But it wouldn't be Maybury. Wherever she went it wouldn't be the same.

Where else would you have to put your car in a compound? Where else would you find someone like big Eva? Someone as nice as Isabella—or Rhannie? Someone as vague as Bruce, or as funny as Hayley?

Where else in the world could there be someone like Harry Brolin?

Blinded by sudden tears, she turned her face to the sea.

The answers to those questions was one and the same. There could never be another Maybury, and there could never be another Harry Brolin. Kirstin knew that, just as she knew she couldn't go back there.

No doubt they were all thinking that her reason for not returning was because of what had happened to her, and as far as she was concerned that was what she would allow them to think.

The truth, of course, was very different. The truth was that she couldn't allow herself to return to work alongside the man she loved and see him resume his relationship with the woman he loved—the woman he had always loved.

It had been a difficult week in more ways than one for she had also told her parents about Scott's letter and his plans to marry.

'Are you upset?' her mother had asked, watching her fearfully.

'Not as much as I once thought I might have been,' she'd replied ambiguously. 'Can you understand that?' she'd asked her mother wearily.

'I'm not sure I understand anything any more,' her mother had replied. Then later, when they were again alone, she'd gone on tentatively to say, 'Kirstin, when we came up to see you, when you were lying there so ill. . .'

'Yes?' she'd replied, dreading what might be about to come.

'Well. . . Harry, Harry Brolin. . .?'

'Yes?' Coolly she'd raised her eyebrows. 'What about him?'

'He seemed. . .he seemed, oh, I don't know, quite distraught, really, by what had happened to you. . .'

'Well, I suppose he would,' she'd replied lightly, while dying inside. 'After all, he was sort of responsible for me. If I'd died there would have been a murder charge—very messy for the practice.'

'Don't!' Her mother had shuddered, then a moment later had gone on to say, 'That wasn't quite what I meant—there seemed more to it somehow. He seemed, I don't know, personally involved somehow. . . Your father and I thought. . .we wondered. . .'

'There's nothing to wonder,' Kirstin had replied firmly, putting paid to the conversation and to any notions her mother might have been harbouring. And at the same time she'd wished that she could put paid to her own pain and longing which, far from going away or even becoming less, was threatening to get the better of her.

That had been that afternoon. Her escape had been now, this evening, to the beach.

She walked right to the water's edge, watching the lacy curl of foam as the waves broke over her shoes. There would be a water mark on the white canvas when they dried, but she didn't care. Putting her arms round her body, she hugged herself tightly—as if drawing comfort from the simple gesture.

The tide would turn soon and start to inch in again and the gulls, swooping and crying overhead, would settle for the night. She watched as a small fishing vessel chugged out of the distant harbour, heading for the open sea, then with a sigh she turned to go.

For a moment she wasn't sure what was different.

Something was. But what?

The sea-wall and the dry sand were still deserted and

the men still dug for bait, but something was different.

Kirstin screwed up her eyes. Hadn't there only been two figures digging bait before?

Now there were three.

Yes, that was it, a third figure had joined the first two but, as Kirstin drew a little closer, she saw that the third figure wasn't digging but was merely watching.

There was something oddly familiar about this third figure, she decided as she made her way along the wet sand towards the little group.

Local man, probably. Someone she'd known since childhood.

But, no, it was more than that.

There was something so familiar about the slightly stocky figure and the almost arrogant stance as to be almost intimate. Even the clothes, the dark jacket and trousers and the high-necked shirt, she recognised as if they were her own.

But—her breath caught in her throat—it couldn't be, not here in Bembridge. He was miles away in Maybury.

He barely even looked up as she approached, only acknowledging her arrival by nodding at the bait-diggers and saying, 'Fascinating business, that.'

'Yes. . .' Kirstin, who had seen it a thousand times before, nodded. 'Yes, I suppose it is.'

He continued to watch for agonising minutes while Kirstin stood alongside him, also apparently watching but with eyes that were unseeing, her brain teeming with questions.

At last he drew away and as if by mutual consent they began to walk, away from the bait-diggers and along the expanse of wet sand.

'This is really quite something.' He paused for a moment, staring out to sea and taking in deep lungfuls of the fresh evening air.

'How did you know where I was?' she managed to say at last.

'I saw your mother,' he said, turning back to her. 'She told me I would find you down here. I gather this is a favourite spot of yours?'

'Yes.' She nodded. 'I always brought the dogs down here in the evenings.'

'But not tonight?'

'I'm sorry?'

'You didn't bring the dogs with you tonight?'

'No.' She shook her head. 'I thought if I did that my mother would come as well. . . I needed some time alone.'

'And now I've ruined that. . .' he said softly.

She wanted to say that, yes, he had ruined it, not only her time alone but her whole life. Instead, she just shrugged and remained silent.

'I got your letter,' he said at last.

'Yes.' She waited, expecting him to say more but he didn't. In the end she said, 'I can't think why you've come. I thought I explained everything in the letter.'

'No,' he said, 'you didn't explain anything in the letter.'

'Oh, but I—'

'Not that I can't understand your reasons for not wanting to come back,' he interrupted. 'After all, it hasn't exactly been a picnic for you.'

'I never expected it to be,' she said flatly. 'You warned me it wouldn't be easy. Right at the start you warned me.'

'Even so. . .'

'You gave me a month. . .you said that was all I would last.'

'Well, I was wrong there. You are obviously made of sterner stuff than I thought.' He paused then went on, 'But I guess everyone has their breaking point and I can't say I blame you—what with a stabbing, a body fished out of the water, break-ins and a fractured skull into the bargain.' He paused again. 'And then, as if all that wasn't enough, you've had me going on at you all the time, putting you down over your attitudes towards housing, medical procedures, social problems, family life—just about everything, really.'

There was a long silence before he added, 'Like I say, it doesn't surprise me that you've chosen not to come back.

On the other hand. . .it beats me how you can prefer all this sea air and civilised living to the pollution and tensions of dear old Maybury.'

'So, why are you here, Harry?' she asked quietly at last, ignoring his attempt at humour.

'To try to persuade you to change your mind.'

'No.'

'Why not?' There was a raw edge to his tone.

'Because I don't want to.'

'Are you afraid?'

'No.' She shook her head and gazed out to sea. The little fishing boat had stopped, far out, casting its nets.

'Then why? I don't understand.'

'I have my reasons,' she said.

'Will you tell me them?'

His voice was gentle now, but how could she tell him? How could she say what those reasons were?

But maybe she should. Maybe she quite simply should turn to him and say, I can't come back, Harry, because I'm in love with, and because I'm in love with you I just couldn't bear to work alongside you and see you with Juliet.

Furthermore, I couldn't bear not to share our Sunday mornings any more, not to go for a drink together or to have early morning breakfast at a road stall after a police call-out—all those little things that have come to mean so much.

And how could I bear it, knowing that Juliet is in your apartment at night?

How could I bear it when you eventually marry her, as you surely will?

She half turned to him, as if she might from somewhere find the courage to say those things. But she was never to know because Harry spoke first.

'I don't know what it would take to make you change your mind,' he said, 'but would it make a difference if I was to ask you to marry me?'

A P&O ferry far out on the horizon chose that moment to sound its horn and Kirstin thought she had misheard him. She turned slowly as the sound of the horn sank into an echo.

'What did you say?' she said.

'I asked you to marry me,' he said quietly.

'I thought that was what you said,' she said slowly, 'but I decided I must have made a mistake.'

'Why should you think that?'

'It was so unlikely. . .'

'Why?'

'When someone asks someone to marry them it's usually because they are in love.'

'That's true,' he agreed.

'You don't even like me, Harry.'

'I don't know what gave you that idea.'

She took a deep breath, fighting for control. 'For a start you disagree with everything I say—and you can't deny that,' she said quickly, 'because you practically admitted as much just now.'

'That doesn't mean I don't like you,' he replied abruptly. 'Neither does it give any reason to suppose I couldn't love you.'

'Maybe.' She shrugged. 'So try this. How can you want to marry me when you're in love with someone else?'

He stopped then and when Kirstin turned to look at him she found that he was staring at her in apparent amazement. 'Who says I'm in love with someone else?'

She shrugged again. 'It appears to be common knowledge in Maybury.'

'Is that so?' He raised surprised eyebrows. 'And the identity of the lady in question—is that also common knowledge?'

'It might be.' She struggled to appear casual but was only too aware that her heart was pounding so uncomfortably that it threatened to suffocate her.

Harry was silent for a moment then, thrusting his hands into his trouser pockets, he hunched his shoulders in a defensive gesture. 'Any moment now you're going to tell me it's Val Metcalf.'

'Oh, so you are aware of Val's feelings?' Kirstin raised her eyebrows in sudden amusement.

'Of course I am,' he muttered. 'I'm not that insensitive. It's just that I've chosen not to aggravate that particular situation in case it gets out of hand.'

He remained stubbornly silent for a while as they continued to walk then he said, 'Don't get me wrong. I'm sure Val is a lovely lady, but she isn't. . .'

'Juliet?' said Kirstin softly. 'Was that what you were going to say, Harry?' she asked when he threw her a sharp glance. 'That she isn't Juliet?'

'No,' he said, 'I wasn't, I was going to say Val isn't for me. But is that what all this is about? Juliet?'

'I don't know,' Kirstin replied, still casually, she hoped. 'You tell me.'

He was silent again then said curiously, 'Who told you about Juliet?'

'Estelle told me some, and some I learnt from talk at the centre.'

'So, what exactly were you told?'

'That Juliet was the love of your life. . .'

He sucked in his breath sharply.

'That you were engaged at one time and seemed set to marry. . .'

'And then. . .?' There was a rough edge to his voice now.

'That Juliet met Paul and married him, but that you never got over it. That you are a one-woman man and that woman is Juliet.'

He gave a sudden, short, bark of a laugh that made Kirstin jump. 'So that's what they say, is it?'

'But is it true?'

He shrugged. 'For a time, maybe it was. But things change. You came along. . .'

'But, if you felt something for me, why didn't you say?' Suddenly she felt a swift stab of exasperation.

He shrugged. 'You made it plain you didn't like me and, besides, I thought you were tied up with your yachtsman. I didn't want to ruin things for you. . .'

'It's all off with Scott,' she said and, seeing his quick look of surprised pleasure, added, 'In fact, now that I think about it I'm not sure it was ever really on. . .'

'You mean you aren't going to marry him after all?'

'No. . .I don't think I ever was. . .'

They walked again for a time in silence, leaving the wet sand behind and climbing over a steep bank of stones, dried seaweed, cuttlefish and smooth, bleached pieces of driftwood twisted into tortured shapes and washed in by the tide.

'You still haven't told me why you don't want to come back,' he said at last, taking her hand and helping her over the uneven surface.

'Estelle told me about Juliet and Paul's divorce.'

Harry frowned. 'I can't see what that has to do with anything. . .'

'She also said that as far as she was concerned they should never have got married. That Juliet had only ever really loved one man and that was you. . . Then she said that she didn't feel it was too late for the pair of you.'

'So why should that affect your decision?' He was staring at her now and Kirstin found herself unable to meet his gaze.

'I couldn't bear it,' she mumbled, turning her head so that her words were almost taken out to sea by the breeze.

'You couldn't bear what?' There was a note of urgency in his voice now.

'Seeing you and Juliet together. . .' She turned back to him. 'Standing by and watching the pair of you get married, possibly living in the apartment. . .'

'Can I take it from that that you may have feelings for me after all?'

'Oh, Harry.' She stopped and looked at him—at the rugged, uneven features, the unusual tawny-coloured eyes and the dark shadow on his jaw—and her breath caught in her throat. 'Of course I have. I think I always have. . .right from that very first day. All the arguing just made it more intense somehow. . .'

'I thought you couldn't stand the sight of me.' His voice was suddenly husky with emotion.

'You made me angry at times, Harry,' she said, 'I'll grant you that. I thought you were arrogant and self-opinionated and, I must admit, my heart sank when I learnt you were taking over as my trainer, but then. . .'

'Then?' he said gently and stopped, taking her other hand and looking into her eyes. 'What then?'

'I suppose I began to see another side of you. I realised you did care about people and about injustices. . . I even at times wondered if you did care about me. . .'

'What times?' he murmured.

'That night in your flat.' Her voice was little more than a whisper now as he drew even closer and the scent of him mingled with that of the sea air.

'When I did this?' Bending his head, he gently kissed

her lips and she tasted the salt before he drew back.

'Yes—' she nodded '—and there were other times. . .our Sunday mornings, the late night calls. . . But then,' she went on shakily, 'when Estelle came to see me in hospital and said what she did I decided I must have imagined it all.'

'No, Kirstin,' he said, 'you didn't imagine it. And Estelle is wrong, you know. Quite wrong.'

'Is she?' Hardly daring to hope, she looked into his eyes.

'Yes. She was quite right about how I once felt about Juliet. And, yes, I thought it was the end of my world when she married Paul. For a time it probably was, but I gradually came to realise that it was also the end of my love for her. It's in the past, Kirstin. I could never feel that way about Juliet again.'

'Does she know that?'

'She does now,' he said briefly.

'So, did she think there was a chance you and she could resume where you left off all those years ago?'

'I think she wondered if it might be possible. But when I made it plain it was out of the question she accepted it, and even seemed to agree with me that you can't turn the clock back. We are both different people now. Do you understand, Kirstin? Do you know what I'm trying to say?'

'I think so,' she whispered, reaching up her hand and gently running it down the side of his cheek, 'but say it again anyway.'

'I love you,' he said, his voice husky again. 'I want to marry you. I want us to spend the rest of our lives together.'

'Before I answer,' she said, her heart bursting now with love for him, 'there's something I need to know.'

'Yes? Anything.'

She took a deep breath. 'That night in your apartment. . .'

'Yes. . .?'

'Where did you sleep?'

'What do you mean—where did I sleep? Where do you think I slept?'

'Did you sleep on the sofa, Harry?'

'What do you think?' There was a wicked glint now in his eyes.

'I don't know,' she said. 'Honestly, I don't know. I must have been so tired that I. . . Anyway, that's why I'm asking. . . I need to know.'

'Is that so?' He chuckled. 'Tell you what,' he said, 'I'll make a bargain with you, Kirstin, my love. Marry me, and I'll tell you on our wedding night.'

Gathering her into his arms, his lips closed over hers and as desire leapt inside her quite suddenly she realised that it didn't matter to her at all where he had slept that night.

What did matter was where he would be sleeping in the future—every night for the rest of their lives.

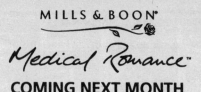

MILLS & BOON®

Medical Romance™

COMING NEXT MONTH

I'D LOVE A BABY! by Margaret Barker

Jenni Dugdale wanted a baby! And Dr Carl Devine offered to father the baby and leave Jenny to bring up the baby on her own. The natural way was surely the best, and Jenni willingly agreed. But then she wanted Carl to stay and play the part of father *and* husband!

DOCTOR'S DILEMMA by Sheila Danton

Serina Grant's holiday in Canada was to help her overcome her mother's death. Then she met Greg Pardoe and the attraction was instant. But he would only have a casual fling and she refused. There was only one solution—but it was all up to Greg...

A SPECIALIST'S OPINION by Lilian Darcy

Summer moved to Bermuda to be with her fiance. But shortly after her arrival the engagement ended. So Summer plunged herself into her work—and that meant close contact with the attractive Randall Macleay. Then he found out why she had broken with her fiancé...

WINGS OF DEVOTION by Meredith Webber
Flying Doctors

Kelly Jackson arrived at the base and announced that she was Colin Forbes, Jack Gregory's new locum! Colin was on his honeymoon and she was his replacement. Jack found Kelly infuriating and intriguing. But they both carried baggage from the past...

FOUR FREE
specially selected
Medical Romance™ novels
__PLUS__ a FREE Mystery Gift
when you return this page...

Return this coupon and we'll send you 4 Medical Romance novels and a mystery gift absolutely FREE! We'll even pay the postage and packing for you.

We're making you this offer to introduce you to the benefits of the Reader Service™– FREE home delivery of brand-new Medical Romance novels, at least a month before they are available in the shops, FREE gifts and a monthly Newsletter packed with information, competitions, author profiles and lots more...

Accepting these FREE books and gift places you under no obligation to buy, you may cancel at any time, even after receiving just your free shipment. Simply complete the coupon below and send it to:

MILLS & BOON READER SERVICE, FREEPOST, CROYDON, SURREY, CR9 3WZ.

READERS IN EIRE PLEASE SEND COUPON TO PO BOX 4546, DUBLIN 24

NO STAMP NEEDED

Yes, please send me 4 free Medical Romance novels and a mystery gift. I understand that unless you hear from me, I will receive 4 superb new titles every month for just £2.20* each, postage and packing free. I am under no obligation to purchase any books and I may cancel or suspend my subscription at any time, but the free books and gift will be mine to keep in any case. (I am over 18 years of age)

M7YE

Ms/Mrs/Miss/Mr_____
BLOCK CAPS PLEASE

Address_____

_____

_____ Postcode _____

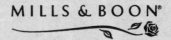

MILLS & BOON®

In Sultry New Orleans,
Passion and Scandal are...

Unmasked

Mills & Boon are delighted to bring you a star studded
line-up of three internationally renowned authors in one
compelling volume—

Janet Dailey

Elizabeth Gage

Jennifer Blake

Set in steamy, sexy New Orleans, this fabulous collection of
three contemporary love stories centres around one magical
night—the annual masked ball.

Disguised as legendary lovers, the elite of New Orleans are
seemingly having the times of their lives.
Guarded secrets remain hidden—until midnight...
when *everyone* must unmask...

Available: August 1997   Price: £4.99